MACONAQUAH'S STORY

MACONAQUAH' S STORY

"The Saga of Frances Slocum"

By
Kitty Dye

InChem Publishing

Publisher's Cataloging in Publication
(Prepared by Quality Books Inc.)

Dye, Kitty.
  Maconaquah's story: the saga of Fraces Slocum/by Kitty Dye

  p. cm.
  LCCN: 96-765780
  ISBN 0-9642058-2-3

  1. Slocum, Frances 1773-1847. 2. Miami Indians--History. 3. Indian Captivies--United States. I. Title.

E99.M48D94 1996   973'.04'97
                                QBI96-40066

DEDICATION

This book is dedicated to the Miami Indian descendants of Frances Slocum. They have been tribal leaders since her time, and they hold her life among the Miamis in great esteem.

Kitty Dye

The portrait of Maconaquah opposite, and the other pictures reproduced in this book were taken from "Indians and a Changing Frontier - the Art of George Winter." Published by the Indiana Historical Society and the Tippecanoe County Historical Association in 1993. Compiled by Sarah E. Cooke and Rachael Ramaghyani. These pictures are used with permission.

George Winter wrote that: *"Frances Slocum presented a very singular and picturesque appearance. Her toute en semble was unique. She was dressed in a red calico 'shirt', figured with large shewy yellow and green, folded within the upper part of a 'metta coshee', or petticoat of black cloth of excellent quality. Her nether limbs were clothed with fady-red leggings, 'winged' with green ribbons, and her feet were moccasinless."*

'Kick-ke-se-quah', her daughter, who seemed not to be without some pride in her mother's appearing to the best advantage, placed a black silk shawl over her shoulders - pinning it in front.

I made no suggestions of any change in these arrangements, but left the toilette uninfluenced in any one particular.

Frances placed her feet across the lower round of the chair, and her hands fell upon her lap in good position."

Maconaquah by George Winter
Tippecanoe County Historical Association, Lafayette, Indiana.
Gift of Mrs. Cable G. Ball

ACKNOWLEDGMENTS

Dr. Stewart Rafert, for resource materials, encouragement, and his critique of the early draft of this manuscript.

Shaun Granum, Assistant Curator, Miami County Historical Society, Peru, Indiana.

Sara Beth Terrell, Archivist, Earlham College, Richmond, Indiana.

Lois Skillman, Erie County Historian, Sandusky, Ohio.

Burt Logan, Executive Director, Wyoming Historical and Geological Society, Wilkes-Barre, Pennsylvania.

William H. Siener, former Director, Wyoming Historical and Geological Society, Wilkes-Barre, Pennsylvania.

Brian Dunnigan, Executive Director, Old Fort Niagara Association, Inc., Youngstown, New York.

Heather Davis, Librarian at the Minnetrista Cultural Center, Muncie, Indiana.

Joyce Miller, Archivist at the Miami (Indiana) County Historical Society and Museum, Peru, Indiana

Special thanks to my "agent" Isaac Tripp, X; Paul Beaudry;

Virginia Colahan and Carol Klohn for their help in turning this story into a real, live book.

I want to extend thanks, also, to the team of Bob and Andy Tubessing. Bob designed the book covers as well as the renditions of the Indian artifacts used throughout the text, and Andy drew all the clear, concise maps.

Mary Anthrop's assistance is also greatly appreciated. Being Archivist at the Tippecanoe County Historical Association, she was instrumental in helping me acquire the George Winter pictures and journal, which I felt would be important contributions to the story.

FOREWARD

The story of Frances Slocum continues to be retold a hundred years after her death. On the one hand, it is the heartwrenching tale of a five year old child taken from a large and loving family., to be miraculously discovered as an old woman. On the other hand, it is the story of complete acculturation to Indian ways. Today, about 1,200 Miami Indians, 20% of the Indiana Miami tribe, are descendants of Frances Slocum. The 10% of the descendants belonging to the Bundy clan are among the most culturally conservative of the seven or so large Miami lineages. For them, Frances Slocum continues to cause unease, because she focuses the attention of European-Americans on them, an often undesired intrusion. As recently as 1964, the Slocum family attempted to get Congress to pass legislation to return the remains of Frances Slocum to Wilkes-Barre, Pennsylvania, which seemed insensitive to the Miami, who defeated the effort.

Frances Slocum's daughter Ozashinquah (ca. 1810-1877) was married five times, and had children by all of her husbands. Ozashinquah, who never spoke English to the end of her life, kept the 810 acres of treaty land she owned east of Peru, Indiana. A Miami tradionalist, she passed her beliefs on to her many children who married all the Miami clans or lineages. As Mrs. Dye points out, it was her son Camillus Bundy (Pimyotamah, The Sound of Something Passing By) who organized the Miami Nation, the modern tribal organization. To defend tribal rights, he sold many beautiful Miami items which today grace the collections of the Detroit Institute of Art, the Museum of the American Indian, and the Cranbrook Institute, Bloomfield Hills,

Michigan.

Today, the Eastern or Miami blend tribal traditions with modern ways of life. Frances Slocum was but one of several captives living among the tribespeople in the 1830s. Descendants of the other captives sometimes resent the attention bestowed upon her by non-indians. At the same time, because of the long time period between her capture and her discovery, and the contrast between the five year old child and the old Indian woman discovered by her family, the story of Frances Slocum remains a classic captivity epic, and one that will continue to be retold. Mrs. Dye's book is a fine addition to the Maconaquah cycle and should encourage others to discover the Miami Indians.

Stewart Rafert

PROLOGUE

Jonathan Slocum had a tough decision to make. If he stayed in Rhode Island he would have to help the colonists in their war for independence from the English King. If he refused, he risked being labelled a Tory, and those who were loyal to the British throne were being driven north to Canada to live. He was not a Tory, of course, but his Quaker beliefs would not permit him to kill another person, no matter how just the cause.

When the shooting war broke out in nearby Concord, Massachusetts in 1775, Jonathan made his decision. He would move his family away from the coastal area where the war would be fought. Remembering the Susquehanna River Valley in the Pennsylvania wilderness he had visited many years before, Johnathan returned there with enough money to buy several properties in the new townships of Putnam and Wilkes-Barre.

Many families were relocating there to escape the war and the crowded conditions in the eastern cities, since the recent eviction of the Delaware Indians from the valley they had called Maugh-waw-wame, meaning Large Plains. The settlers pronounced it "Wyoming." With Forts Wyoming and Forty Fort nearby for protection and the river for easy transportation, Jonathan was confident this was the ideal place to raise his family. A blacksmith by trade, he could see a need for his craft in this frontier settlement.

In the autumn of 1777, Jonathan moved his wife, Ruth, and their nine children, into a two-story log house on the corner of North and Back Streets in the new town of Wilkes-Barre. They were accompanied by Ruth's father, Isaac

Tripp. While the "streets" were just wagon paths, with forest and swamp beyond, the flats were close enough to grow food and pasture the cattle. There was also a shed on the property where Jonathan could set up his forge. This three-acre lot, Number 50 in the town plat, suited their needs, although most of the other families were nearer Fort Wyoming, a half-mile away. Forty Fort was across the river.

The Indians, too, had important decisions to make about whether to help the colonists or the British in their war. The British were favored since they weren't the ones continually pushing the Indians westward. They also paid well for the Indians' furs. Now that the Indians were dependent on the white man for tools, weapons, firewater, and clothing, they were always looking for the best bargain.

The American colonial government was not able to supply the Indians during the Revolutionary War although they made promises to do so in an effort to keep the Indians on their side. The treaty of 1775 stated the Ohio River would be the western boundary of white settlements. Another treaty three years later promised the Delaware that the Americans would establish a fourteenth state just for Indians when they won the war. It would be headed by the Delawares themselves, with representation in Congress.

The Turkey and Turtle clans of the Delaware, who had formerly lived in the Wyoming Valley, were now living in villages along the tributaries of the Ohio River and Lake Erie. They believed the colonists' promises. The Wolf clan lived along the Otsandoske (Sandusky) River, which emptied into Lake Erie. Their Chief Hopacan, or Captain Pipe, didn't believe the promises. He thought the colonial government pretended to be friends of the Delaware so they could seize their lands and destroy them. Other Delaware tribes siding with the British preferred to live near the protection of forts on the shores of the Great Lakes.

One principal fort was on Lake Ontario, at the mouth of the Niagara River. From here, British soldiers and their Indian allies made devastating raids on the frontier settlements in Pennsylvania and New York. On July 3, 1778, word came to the settlers of the Wyoming Valley that British Major John Butler's Rangers and their Indians were on the warpath and were moving toward them. Many families moved into the forts for protection.

Jonathan Slocum's son, Giles, was nineteen when he was faced with the most important decision of his life. If he joined the local militia to help fight off the attack, he would be banned from attending the Quakers' prayer meetings. He would also be shunned by the other Quaker families in the valley. The very real threat to the lives of all the settlers decided him. He knew he could not remain idle while his friends defended his family and him.

Giles enlisted in the militia and bravely fought both Indians and Rangers. Perhaps he wore the traditional big-brimmed hat of the Quakers on that fateful day, for the Indians were quick to notice that a man claiming to be their friend was shooting at them. That "deceit" angered them enough to find out who that person was and how to get revenge.

The truce was signed the next afternoon at Forty Fort. Four months later the Indians returned. This is the true story of the revenge that changed a young girl's life forever.

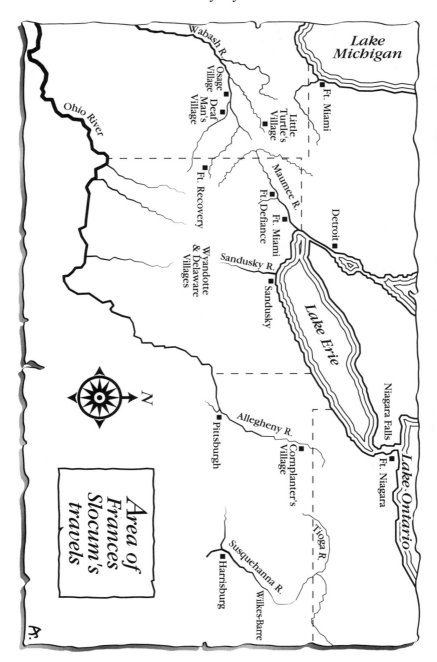

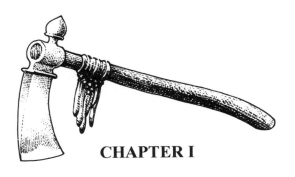

CHAPTER I

THE ABDUCTION OF FRANCES SLOCUM

Three Delaware Indians crouched silently at the edge of the forest and watched the cabin across the road, noticing every detail. They were confident the men inside, who wore the big black hats, would soon leave to work in the nearby field, where corn and pumpkins were ripening fast in the early November chill. While they were busy harvesting, the Indians would have time to reach the house, take or kill the people inside, and be back in the woods before the men could get within shooting range.

This family had red-haired children, Chief Tuck Horse noticed. Good, very good! Red-haired children were highly prized. Smiling to himself, the Chief mused that stealing the children would be even more worthwhile than killing them. He would please his people by bringing back white children to be adopted by families whose own children had died. Tuck Horse instructed the others to each grab a child to take back to their village. This plan was turning out to be well worth the distance they had traveled from his village far to the north.

Tuck Horse's anger was deep. He had been looking forward to revenge on this family of Quakers who claimed to be friends of Indians. One from this house had joined the soldiers during their raid last summer. Grimly he remembered how he was nearly hit by a bullet from the gun of the man wearing the big hat. Not only do these people speak with a forked tongue, he thought, but they have no right to be here. We were promised this land, to be ours forever, when we left the land of the great waters. It is ours.

After that July raid, many settlers in the Wyoming Valley had loaded their wagons and headed back east, but Jonathan and Ruth Slocum had decided to stay. The wagon trip would have been too hard for Ruth, who was expecting a baby soon. Besides, their blacksmith shop was needed, and their first crop of vegetables, along with berry bushes and fruit trees, was doing well in the fertile soil.

"The Indians know us to be peaceable and will bring us no harm," Jonathan reassured his family. "The attackers were from the north, I am told. Surely they will not come back. We must have faith."

To further bolster his courage, Jonathan added, "This land is good. The seed grows well and we will have plenty for the winter. If we went back to Rhode Island, we would have no food of our own. It would be a hardship for neighbors to share with us. We will stay."

Now, four months later, the Indians, patiently watching the house, were not interested in Jonathan Slocum's Quaker philosophy. This was war, and the men of the big hats must go!

Within the house, Jonathan Slocum made plans for the day. "It would please me, William, if thee would work with us today," Jonathan informed his second son. "We have much to do before the ground freezes."

William was delighted to join Giles, Father, and Grandfather in doing men's work in the fields. But along with strict obedience, he had been taught traditional emotional control, so he merely murmured, "It would please me, too, Father."

"And, Ebenezer, thee must help thy mother," Jonathan ordered his twelve-year-old son.

Ebenezer did not allow his disappointment to show. He had been lame ever since a cart had run over his feet when he was a small child, but he did what he could without complaint.

"The Kingsley boys can be watch today and signal us if need be," Jonathan added. Since their father had been abducted by Indians some time ago, Nathan and Wareham Kingsley, along with their mother, had been too frightened to stay by themselves. They had been welcomed into Jonathan and Ruth's household.

Adjusting their big hats more firmly down around their ears, the four men left the house. After getting tools and a wagon from the shed, they were soon at work in their field, well out of sight of the house.

Since they had to be outside anyway, the Kingsley boys decided to sharpen their knives. So engrossed were they at the grindstone that they didn't see the Indians sprint across the road and over the fence until it was too late. A shot rang out. Nathan fell. One of the Indians held Wareham while the others gathered up the knives and scalped poor Nathan.

Ruth ran to the front door when she heard the shot. Realizing what was happening, she bolted the door and grabbed baby Jonathan.

"Run fast and hide in the swamp!" she cried out to the

others in the house as she led them to the back door. Ten-year-old Mary took two-year-old Joseph from her mother's arms and sprinted out the door and over the fence. When she came to the road she hesitated, then turned toward the fort. Running as fast as she could, she thought, "I must get help!"

Ebenezer looked for a place to hide in the house since he knew he could not run fast enough to escape an Indian. He grabbed five-year-old Frances, who was hiding in a corner, too frightened to move, and pulled her under the steps with him, covering them both with some quilts.

The Indians knew they would have to move fast now, as the shot would surely have been heard in the field, as well as at the fort. Entering the house, two of them searched downstairs while one dashed up the steps to the loft to see if anyone was hiding in the bedclothes.

Coming back down, he saw a little foot sticking out of the bundles at the bottom. Jubilantly he shouted to the others as he pulled the frightened children from their hiding place. Now, with Wareham, they had their three captives. Throwing the children over their shoulders, the Indians dashed from the house toward the safety of the woods.

Forgetting her own fear, Ruth ran from her hiding place toward them, screaming, "No! No, please don't take the children!"

Miraculously, she had gotten the Indian's attention and they stopped for a moment. Pointing to Ebenezer's feet, Ruth begged, "The boy is lame. He can do thee no good."

Perhaps realizing a lame child might slow their flight, they dropped Ebenezer to the ground before they disappeared silently into the trees. The men had run from the field as soon as they had heard the shot, but were too late to stop the three Indians with their captive children. Hysterically, Ruth pointed to the place where they had entered the forest.

"Indians have Frances! Go after them, Jonathan. Bring Frances back before they kill her! They went in right there. They can't be far. Oh, do hurry!"

As the men ran into the woods, Ruth stood wringing her hands while tears streamed down her cheeks. Then, suddenly remembering little Jonathan and the others hiding in the swamp, she ran back to where she had left them.

The shot had also been heard at the fort. The leader of the militia, Colonel Zebulon Butler, immediately sent out a squad of soldiers to investigate. Soon, they came upon Mary, nearly exhausted, but still running, still carrying Joseph.

"Indians," she managed to pant, pointing back to the Slocum house.

The soldiers came upon the property at the same time that the women and children scrambled out of the thicket bordering the marsh. The soldiers were preparing to fire their muskets at what they thought were the Indian raiders when Ruth emerged. One soldier stayed behind to guard the women, while the others followed the Slocum men into the forest to try to find the trail of the Indians.

It was obvious the Indians were in a hurry for, they had left a trail that was easy to follow. They had taken the path along the woods directly to the Susquehanna River, then along the bank as close to the water as possible. The trackers found footprints in the soft ooze as well as some strands of Frances' bright hair which had been caught on a low branch. Suddenly, the trail ended.

After scanning some minutes, the leader of the militia squad finally stated, "They must've crossed the river here. They're probably heading up Abraham Creek, and we'll never find 'em if they get far into those hills. Full'a caves, too, it is." He turned to another man. "Charlie, get back to the fort, on the double, and bring us a boat and any men you can scare up."

Giles was all for swimming across the river, since the Indians had apparently done so. He reasoned that the water level was low enough at that time of year to practically wade across.

The leader responded slowly, "I wouldn't recommend it, Mr. Slocum, unless you'd rather catch pneumonia than your sister. Them Indians is tougher than we are. Chances are they have dry clothes stashed away somewheres close."

Although it seemed an eternity to the Slocum men, it wasn't long before three boats paddled up the river toward them, with eight more men to help in the search.

Once across, they divided into two teams, in order to cover both sides of the creek. The going was difficult through dense undergrowth. Thorns and muck covered rocky ledges and dangerous crevices.

After two futile hours of hunting for signs that the Indians had passed by, the leader signaled it was time to stop and turn around. It was dangerous to venture too far from the fort.

"We'll search this shoreline more carefully tomorrow," he promised. "Maybe they went in somewheres else."

They did hunt the next day, and the day after that, but found no signs of the Indians or their captives.

"Thee just can't give up," pleaded Ruth when Col. Butler told her the hunt was being called off. "The poor child didn't even have her shoes on. "Oh, why didn't I let her wear them that day?"

"Now, don't blame thyself, Ruth," consoled Jonathan. "You know shoes have to be saved for prayer meeting and special occasions. Thee had no way of knowing Frances would need them on her feet that morning." He patted her shoulder. "Don't thee worry. We're not giving up the hunt for Frances. We're just postponing it until it's safer to travel. And I've heard the Indians take good care of the white children they take. Even treat 'em special, like part of their families. We must have faith the Lord will look after her until we can find her, that's all."

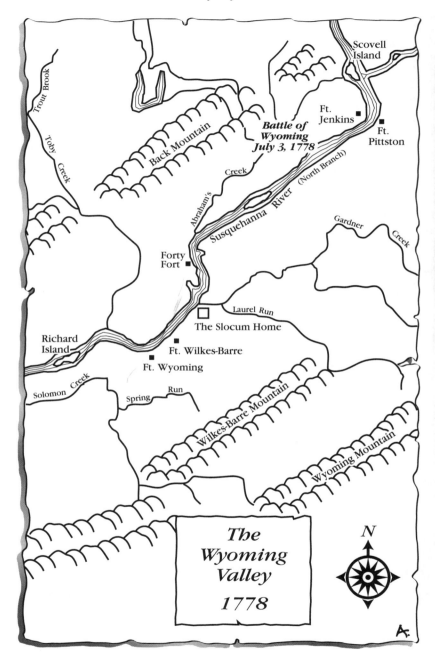

The Wyoming Valley 1778

CHAPTER II

FRANCES TURNS INTO AN INDIAN

Frances pulled the smelly robe about her tightly, huddling into it as much as she could. Even though it smelled bad, it did keep out the damp chill in the cave room where the Indians had led them. She looked at Wareham. He, too, was huddled in his robe, but his eyes were tightly shut.

As if sensing Frances was looking at him, Wareham opened his eyes and stared back at her. Frances could see the tears welling up and falling down his cheeks.

"They killed Nathan," he whispered.

The Indian nearest to him quickly flashed a knife in Wareham's face, muttering, No talk. Kill.

Wareham buried his head in his robe as the Indian repeated the threat to Frances. No talk. Kill.

Frances closed her eyes as tightly as she could. Maybe if she fell asleep this would all be gone, like a bad dream, when she woke.

Someone poked her. She opened her eyes to see an Indian holding out a pouch of what looked like dried corn. By his actions she understood that he was asking her if she wanted some. She had learned to hate that dried food on the wagon trip from their other home and, during the long weeks until their first crops came in. Her look of disgust seemed to amuse the Indian. He offered some to Wareham, who also shook his head in refusal.

The Indians had just started to eat when sounds were heard outside. Instantly, Frances and Wareham had dirty hands clamped over their mouths and knife blades were held inches from their eyes. The menacing Indians didn't have to say, "Kill." The meaning was well understood by their look.

Frances heard her father's voice through the openings high in the stone of the cave, which let in the light. She didn't recognize the other voices, but she knew they had found the Indians' trail and were very near. Her eyes caught Wareham's in a look of hope. They would be rescued now!

As the minutes went by and the voices faded, Frances realized they hadn't found the trail - because the Indians hadn't left one. She remembered her father telling her, "If you want to hide your trail, walk in a stream." The Indians had walked in a stream before coming to this cave. Overcome with grief, Frances no longer cared what the Indians said or did. She threw herself down on the cold, hard stone and cried bitterly.

She must have slept, since she felt so limp when the Indian shook her and sat her up. The room was much dimmer. The Indian who seemed to be the leader was sitting cross-legged in front of her with a pleased expression on his face. In his hand he held two small moccasins. He motioned for her to put out her feet. Tucked into the fur robe, her feet were warm enough, but she thought she had better do what he wanted. She stuck out one foot. The soft piece of deerskin fitted her foot very well. The Indian tied it with a leather thong and waited for a sign of approval.

Frances didn't know what to do. Her mother had taught her to appreciate a gift, but this was different. She wondered what her mother would tell her to do now. Well, her mother wasn't here, so Frances just gave him a very small smile.

Very pleased, the Indian motioned for her other foot. When the second moccasin was tied in place, he helped Frances to her feet so the others could admire the effect of his handiwork.

They had made Wareham a pair of moccasins, too, Frances noticed. He sat on a stone eating some of the dried corn.

"You'd best eat some, Frances," he told her. "The way they're gathering up their things, I've an idea we'll move on as soon as it's dark."

"We can talk now?" Frances asked quietly.

"The Indians have been talking - even laughing," he told her. "It's not likely the searchers will be back this way again today."

Wareham was right. At twilight, the Indians led their prisoners out of the cave and into the stream. Walking carefully, they followed it until total darkness fell. Then they sat on a log by the bank until the moonlight became bright enough for them to continue.

They walked a long time, resting only occasionally. About the time the moonlight disappeared into the trees, they came to a place along the bank, for which the Indians seemed to have been looking. Finding their path, they walked through the trees to a clearing where horses were tied.

With both children astride the horses, the Indians walked

them carefully along a trail, single-file, the rest of the night. As the eastern skies started to lighten, the Indians stopped. Tethering the horses, they climbed under a rocky ledge along with the captives and food supplies. They rested and ate, with one Indian always on guard, for the rest of the day. Traveling again by the fading light of day, and then by moonlight, they arrived at an Indian village sometime during the night.

They stayed at the village for many days in the wigwam of the village chief, his wife, some children, and some very old people. Frances learned the Indian who had first carried her away from home and then made her moccasins, was called Chief Tuck Horse. He could understand English, although he couldn't speak it very well.

Frances and Wareham stayed close to the fire that always burned in the middle of this big place. They didn't like so many Indians always staring at them, sometimes pointing, sometimes laughing. They were sure their captors were talking about them, but what were they planning? The Indians didn't look angry or fierce, but Frances and Wareham had heard stories of cruelty and even torture inflicted on prisoners and they were frightened.

During this rest stop, Tuck Horse made the children cups from softened birch bark, which had been molded and then dried well enough to hold a good drink of water. Because of his thoughtfulness, Frances finally found courage to ask Tuck Horse what the other Indians were talking about.

He grinned. "They like you much," he told her. "Say your hair like burning bush."

One day Tuck Horse told the captives that it was time to move on to his village, many days away. This time they all had their own ponies to ride. Scouts told Tuck Horse that there were no searchers on the trail for the captive children, so they were able to travel by daylight, resting in the late afternoon.

At each camp, one Indian made the fire while the others caught game. The game was speared onto sticks, which were set in the ground close enough to the fire to cook the meat. The dried corn was now mixed with water or honey and wrapped in corn husks. These were buried in the fire coals to cook. The Indians gathered hemlock boughs for the children's beds.

Frances looked forward to bedtime. When all was quiet, she could close her eyes and think about her family and home. What were they doing now? She pictured her mother preparing the meals while scolding the little ones for playing. Oh how she missed sleeping with all her brothers and sisters in the loft! If she tried very hard she could almost hear them whispering to each other so their parents wouldn't hear. She cried softly to herself each night until sleep would finally come.

One afternoon Frances became aware of a strange, distant noise. It gradually became louder until it was almost a roar. Tuck Horse pointed to the tree tops, his hand rippling as it descended to the ground. "Great falls near," he told her.

To Frances' amazement, the river they had been following suddenly plunged into a swirling mist, so far down that a rainbow sparkled far below them. The trail continued along the top of the gorge, high above the river, until they finally arrived at Tuck Horse's village.

His encampment was located where the river emptied

into a great lake, beneath the walls of the biggest fort Frances had ever seen. All the Indians stopped what they were doing to greet Tuck Horse and his companions. They smiled and nodded approval as Frances and Wareham rode by.

Tuck Horse's wigwam was warm and smelled good. An Indian woman rose when they entered and came to Frances. "Come, child, sit and eat," she smiled, motioning Frances to a mat by the fire.

Frances had trouble tucking her feet under her, Indian fashion, to sit close by the fire. The Indian woman showed her how. Their soft laughter at her awkwardness turned into warm, friendly smiles for each other.

The Indian woman pointed to herself, saying, "Shee-kee, my name."

Frances repeated it slowly. Then suddenly remembering her manners, she pointed to herself. "Frances Slocum is my name. Pleased to meet thee."

Shee-kee handed Frances a corn cake she'd been cooking on a stone by the fire. It was still hot so Frances nibbled at it, watching Shee-kee turn others. Many more cakes were cooked from batter in an earthenware bowl.

Frances could have eaten more than the three cakes Shee-kee offered, but the Indian woman indicated "no." Frances understood why a short time later when Tuck Horse entered the wigwam with three other Indian men. They brought four rabbits which Shee-kee quickly dressed and fastened onto sticks by the fire.

As the meat sputtered over the flickering flames, Frances' education in the Delaware language began. By the time the rabbits were done, she could repeat ten words without help. Frances found herself as pleased as the Indians obviously were.

It was many days before Frances realized she was not crying herself to sleep anymore. As she closed her eyes, however, she tried remembering the members of her family as they sat around the supper table. There was Mother, Father, Giles, Judith, William, Ebenezer, Mary, Benjamin, Isaac, Joseph, and Grandfather. Baby Jonathan was still in the cradle. It was comforting to picture them, with heads bowed in silent prayer. It wasn't long, though, before Frances couldn't get all the way around the table before sleep came.

Shee-kee taught Frances many things during the cold winter months. After the morning meal was over and the day's supply of wood was gathered, Shee-kee would uncover the pile of dried reeds and let Frances sort them for her needs that day. Sometimes they made baskets or brooms. Frances learned how to weave the flattened cattail stalks into mats for the floor of the wigwam.

The men were often gone. Sometimes Shee-kee told Frances they were hunting for meat with other men from the village, but other times she would just lower her eyes and pretend she didn't understand Frances' question.

When the men returned with a deer, there was much rejoicing and feasting. Shee-kee let Frances help cut the meat into the right portions for drying. Afterward, they scraped the inside of the skin until it was soft enough to form into warm clothing or new moccasins. The bones were saved for tools and the sinew used to lash the hide together for its many uses. Everything on the deer was used.

Frances' favorite time was when Tuck Horse took his

fiddle out of its box and played for them. Shee-kee sometimes sang softly to the music. They explained that Tuck Horse sometimes played for the white people when they were away from the village. For the entertainment, the whites would give him needed supplies or food.

Frances had never heard such beautiful sounds as Tuck Horse could make from those strings. She wondered why her father had said that music, and even games, was a frivolous waste of time. He had always told his children that if they had spare time, it should be spent in prayer or meditation. She was glad Father wasn't here to scold her for humming along and rocking to the music like the Indians did.

One day Shee-kee told Frances that she and Tuck Horse were going to adopt her into their family. Their own daughter, She-let-a-wash, had died many moons ago. Frances would take her place in their hearts and wigwam.

There would be a great feast when the men returned, but first, Frances had to have the proper clothing. Shee-kee fashioned a dress for Frances from the softest deerskin. Colorful ribbons and wampum beads were sewn onto it until Frances thought it the finest dress she had ever seen.

"If only Mary could see me now," she told Shee-kee as she was trying it on one day. Frances tried to tell the Indian woman about the time her older sister had found some beads and hung them around her neck. Mother had found out and angrily told Mary that people who wore such gaudy baubles were to be shunned, since they were more interested in impressing other people than in caring what God thought of them.

Since she was going to be adopted into Tuck Horse's

family, Frances reasoned that she could rightfully dress like an Indian. But what would she wear to go home after she was found? The plain dress she had been wearing when Tuck Horse took her was already too small for her. Frances dreaded the discipline she would be subjected to if her mother and father saw her with ribbons in her hair and beads on her moccasins.

"The moon and stars tell me the Great Spirit is pleased you have come to live with us," Tuck Horse told Frances. "You will bring us much happiness. We grieved when She-let-a-wash died, but now her spirit is in your body and we rejoice. You will be She-let-a-wash and share in our fortunes."

When the day of the adoption came, Shee-kee braided many ribbons into Frances' hair, painted a red circle on each cheek, and gave her a circlet of beautiful wampum to wear around her waist, over the new dress. Proudly, they all walked to the fire circle where the others in the Delaware village were gathering for a feast. While the food cooked, the young people played games the first She-let-a-wash had enjoyed.

After the remains of the feast had been cleared away, the men put on a great dance, circling about the fire, while the women and children sat a short distance from them chanting to the rhythm and beating on the ground with sticks. The new She-let-a-wash was so truly happy she even forgot to look around to see if she could spot Wareham in the crowd.

Back in their wigwam, Tuck Horse told his adopted daughter, "Now we can tell you about the Walam Olum. It is the story of our creation, told by all the Grandfathers from the very beginning. It is even all written down, like the white people do, with red paint on many pieces of bark. It is very long."

With a sharp stick, Tuck Horse drew a half moon shape with lines underneath on the dirt floor by the firepit.

"This is the beginning," he chanted, "of all the Lenni Lenape people. There at the edge of all the water, where the land ends. The fog over the earth was plentiful, and this was where the Great Spirit stayed."

Tuck Horse rubbed out the drawing. "Think on this tonight, daughter. Next night I'll tell you more. It is a good story; a true one. I want you to remember it all as it reveals the answers to all questions in our life."

Shee-kee told her, "Lenni Lenape is the traditional name of our people. We lived by the waters the white people call "Delaware" a long time ago. We came to be known as the Delawares since that time. The name continued even though so many white people came that we had to move west into the valley of the Susquehanna."

When spring came, the Indians moved out of the village to places where they could clear enough land to plant their seeds. When the planting was done, they gathered together for one of their favorite celebrations. In a large, cleared area, dancers sang or shouted as they went around in a circle. Two men beat out the rhythm on drums of hide. Others sat outside the dancing ring, singing and beating the ground with sticks. They implored the Great Spirit to take care of their seeds planted in Mother Earth.

Shee-kee told She-let-a-wash the Indians could not understand how the white people could "own" their own piece of Mother Earth. It was the same to Indians as the air, rain, the sun or moon - to be shared by all people, animals, birds, and fish. How else could they all roam about to get the things they needed?

After the planting ceremony, Tuck Horse told his family they would travel to the land of his brothers while the seeds grew. She-let-a-wash and Shee-kee packed the cooking pots and clothing into strong woven hemp bags and loaded them onto pack horses. Tuck Horse packed his fiddle himself.

Before leaving, Tuck Horse gave She-let-a-wash her own pony to ride and care for. "The pony will serve you well if you treat her as a sister," he told her.

With the great lake, called "Erie" by Tuck Horse, to the north of them, they rode for many days. Her adopted father told She-let-a-wash that long ago a tribe of Erie Indians lived along the shores until the fierce Iroquois chased them away.

"These same Iroquois subjected our people into woman status long ago, but this war between the Long Knives (American colonial soldiers) and their English father enables us to prove our bravery and courage," he said proudly. "We are now so important that both sides of the war need our help." He added that the British commander at the Niagara fort had asked him to make this trip to visit his brothers along the Otsandoske (Sandusky) River to persuade them all to come over to the side of the English. "They'll give our brothers all the supplies they'll need if they do."

Remembering the attack on the settlers on the Susquehanna, She-let-a-wash asked Tuck Horse why he was on the side of the British, who were killing so many colonists. This wasn't the right side, to her way of thinking.

After a long pause, Tuck Horse answered slowly and carefully. "Two times since the white man came to our shores, we have had to move away from our lands. Our cousins, the Shawnee and Wyandot peoples, invited us to live with them on the other side of the mountains, where the land is rich and the game plentiful. We found it so - until the white man followed. First they moved into the hunting grounds that have always been open to all Indians, saying the land was theirs now, and killing our hunters. Then they crossed the great Ohio River, killing our people and burning our homes and food."

"The Chief of the Long Knives says the land belongs to the Indians, but still he allows his people to come. I cannot believe that white man, who speaks with such a forked tongue. No, little daughter, I will not help such a people. Instead, we join the white people whose chief is across the great water, to fight our common enemy."

Presently, they came to a smaller lake with a river leading into it. Tuck Horse called it "Otsandoske."

"The name," he explained, "means clear, cold water, for the many springs to be found along its course. It is a good land. My people would be happy here if the white man would leave them alone."

After a day's ride upstream along the Otsandoske River, they came to Hopacan's village. Hopacan meant, literally, Tobacco Pipe, but he was usually called Captain Pipe. The chief of the Wolf clan greeted them warmly. He was much pleased with the turkey the travelers brought along and set his wife to dressing and preparing it.

After a hearty meal, the brothers talked about Tuck Horse's mission.

"You come at a good time," Captain Pipe told Tuck Horse. "Our brothers of the Turkey and Turtle clans have just returned from a meeting with the Chiefs of the Long Knives. So poor are they, they asked permission to trade with the British at Detroit. 'No,' the Long Knives said. 'We will supply you with the necessities.'"

"More promises that will not be kept," Captain Pipe lamented. "They are indeed in great need and cannot live much longer on promises. I will call a council of my brothers. Maybe you can talk sense into their heads."

At the council, Tuck Horse told the chiefs, "The English father is not pleased that you let the enemy pass through your lands to attack their fort at Detroit. He urges you to take up the hatchet against the Long Knives with your British friends. You will be rewarded with much ammunition and fine goods, befitting the leaders that you are."

Captain John Killbuck, Jr., leader of the Turkey clan, addressed Tuck Horse. "The Long Knives are going to win this great battle against their English father across the waters. We get reports of the many victories over the Red Coats. I have just returned and have seen for myself. General Washington, the men of Congress, and even Colonel Brodhead at Fort Pitt, have promised me the white man will not settle beyond the Ohio River."

"All this land will be an Indian nation when the war is over," Killbuck continued with great dignity. "Our people will be its leader. It is a great dream. White Eyes, chief of the Turtles, died for that dream. I will carry on in his place."

Unable to persuade Killbuck to change his loyalties, Tuck Horse and his family returned to their home by the British fort at the mouth of the Niagara River.

When the fall came and the corn was harvested, the

Indians had another celebration to the Great Spirit as well as to all the lesser gods who helped grow the grain. Then, while the women and girls prepared the corn for winter storage, the men went out on the hunt for deer. The winter months would be spent in preparing the skins for clothing and mocassins, for appliquing ribbon and wampum into adornments and jewelry, and for much storytelling around the wigwam fire. Tuck Horse continued the story of the Walam Olum, telling She-let-a-wash about the beginnings and travels of the Lenni Lenape, from their migration across the seas to the west, to the coming of the white man from the east.

By now, She-let-a-wash was nearly seven years old and had been living as an Indian for over a year. She had adapted so well to her new environment that she made no attempt to attract attention to herself or call for help in encounters with white people, even though a continual flow of people came through the Indian encampment and fort that winter. The visiters were British sympathizers and Indians with their prisoners, who were being chased out of the colonies by angry American colonial soldiers. She-let-a-wash was surprised one day to recognize a cousin, Isaac Tripp, among the prisoners. He was being well treated, and they even talked several times before he was moved on.

It is a matter of public record that on March 2, 1780, a "Hookam child; Kingsley child, November 2, 1775" were listed among fourteen other prisoners who were herded off to Canada along with their Tory families by American Colonels Fred Fisher and John Harper. While the spelling of Frances' name is wrong, as well as the year of their abduction, historians think it was Frances and Wareham, with their respective Indian families.

She-let-a-wash and her family spent the remainder of the war years well within the British territories on the northern side of Lake Erie, ranging as far west as the fort at Detroit. Messengers kept them informed of the action to the south of the lake and their brothers on the Otsandoske. They learned that many of those Indians died during the harsh winter of 1779-1780 while waiting for supplies from the American colonials. The supplies never came.

In spite of Killbuck, Captain Pipe rallied the Turkey and Turtle clans to join his Wolf clan in getting needed goods from the British, and making war on the Americans. To combat them, settlers on the frontier organized a militia to fight off the Indian attacks. They were so incensed with hatred of the Indians that on March 7, 1782, a militia from Pennsylvania attacked the peaceable Moravian Mission of Christianized Indians living at Gnadenhutten Ohio, on the Tuscarawas River. All ninety citizens, men, women and children, were either beaten or burned to death.

The massacre at Gnadenhutten greatly affected nine-year-old She-let-a-wash. She became as embittered against the white people as any of her Indian friends were. She had not only begun to look like an Indian, but was starting to think like one. Frances was well on her way to becoming a real Indian.

Tuck Horse thought that when the Revolutionary War was over, She-let-a-wash's white family might start looking for her. He told her that if she were ever found by her relatives, she would be made to return to the civilization she now hated and distrusted. She-let-a-wash had no desire to live the white man's way, in a white man's world. It was not her way anymore. It was decided that the family would go out west, far from the white frontier, where she would not be found.

The great Miami Village of Kekionga, at the fork of three rivers (the present site of Fort Wayne, Indiana), was a good place for them to go when it was safe to travel. Tuck Horse's family established their wigwam about 12 miles from Kekionga, where they found fertile land to grow enough vegetables and other plants to sustain them throughout the long winter months. Game animals for food and fur were abundant in that plains area, well interspersed with forests and rivers. The animal hides could also be sold to obtain needed supplies. It was a good life.

In the early 1790s, She-let-a-wash married a Delaware Indian but, for some reason, the marriage was not a good one. Following Indian custom, Tuck Horse and Shee-kee reclaimed their daughter and banned the unwanted husband from their wigwam.

By this time, the frontier had also arrived at Kekionga. The village was now in the middle of the Northwest Territory, which had been ceded to the American government by a treaty with the British following the Revolutionary War. The Americans wanted to buy out previous treaty claims to the Indian tribes and relocate them west of the Mississippi River, in order to provide land and safety to the settlers who were arriving in the territory in ever-increasing numbers. When the Indians wouldn't sell, American government troops were sent in to capture the leaders and force them to concede to new treaties favorable to the American government.

By combining forces, the Indians defeated two attempts by American troops to overwhelm them in 1790 and 1791. President George Washington then appointed General "Mad Anthony" Wayne to train an army that would defeat the Indians. General Wayne's troops were ready for action in the summer of 1794. He deployed them north from Cincinnati, Ohio, in August, encountering 2,000 combined Chippewa, Delaware, Miami, Mingo, Ottawa, Potawatomi, Shawnee, and Wyandot Indians along the banks of the Maumee River. The date was August 20th. The area was ideal for the Indians, as a recent tornado had felled the trees, making good cover for them to lie in ambush. In spite of that advantage, General Wayne's army defeated the Indians in what has since come to be known as the Battle of Fallen Timbers (located just southwest of present-day Toledo, Ohio).

Word of the disastrous defeat spread quickly throughout the Indian villages. Tuck Horse, Shee-kee, and She-let-a-wash just happened to be close to the area, so the next day they canoed to the battle site, slowly drifting near to the shore.

After beaching their canoe, they walked in shocked disbelief among the fallen trees and dead comrades. Suddenly they heard a moaning sound from a tangle of brush. When they investigated, they found a wounded brave who had managed to hide himself from the marauding troops.

With great difficulty they got him into their canoe where they gave him water and bound his wounds. Although the distance to their wigwam was not far, it took them a very long time to reach it. The wounded man was in great pain and needed to rest frequently along the way. They watched anxiously for enemy scouts, but fortunately, the main army seemed to have gone the other way. It was a long, torturous journey for their poor, wounded passenger. She-let-a-wash did what she could to make him more comfortable with cool cloths and gentle songs.

Once back at the wigwam, where the wounded stranger received the rest and care he needed, he was able to tell them something about himself.

"My name is Shepoconah. I belong to the great Miami nation living along the banks of the Wabash and Mississinewa Rivers, not far from here. We have many villages and many brave chiefs. We are a rich and peaceable people, growing a very fine quality of corn that is much in demand with travelers and traders"

Shepoconah's wounds healed slowly. By the onset of winter, he was trying to walk a little way each day, in the company of She-let-a-wash, but he tired so easily they couldn't go far. It was decided he should remain through the winter and regain his strength before attempting to return to his village.

Sitting before the fire, She-let-a-wash enjoyed talking with Shepoconah and learning about his family. He told her of his many adventures on hunts with other braves to lands far to the west. But when he asked her about her childhood, she would suddenly think of something important she should be doing elsewhere and hurry off. After living for fifteen years as an Indian, she never thought of herself as a white person - unless someone asked an unfortunate question that reminded her of her secret shame. She liked and respected Shepoconah very much. He must never find out that she was really one of those whites they both hated so fiercely.

The winter of 1795 was unusually severe. Even the animals felt it. Those who survived hunkered in, trying to hold out until spring. Not even game would venture forth in such weather, so Tuck Horse's hunting forays were usually futile. With winter still raging and the food supplies almost gone, Shepoconah realized something must be done quickly.

One night, as everyone was sleeping soundly, Shepoconah gathered what he could and crept silently from the wigwam, intent upon doing what he could to help a desperate situation. Miraculously, he arrived at Kekionga many days later nearly frozen and traded what he'd brought with him for food. Then, mustering some hidden strength, he trudged back through the snow to Tuck Horse's wigwam with enough supplies to see them through until spring.

To Shepoconah's way of thinking, his actions were only just. They had saved his life; he must save theirs. Besides, he genuinely liked the family - especially She-let-a-wash. Tuck Horse and Shee-kee were not blind to the obvious affection their guest felt for their daughter nor to the way she seemed to respond to it. In gratitude for his bravery and with a deep belief in their adopted daughter's happiness with such an honorable man, Tuck Horse and Shee-kee gave their blessings to the couples' marriage.

Shepoconah bestowed the name "Maconaquah," meaning Little Bear Woman, on his new bride. In the Miami tongue, the name stood for skill and bravery in riding a horse. The couple remained with Tuck Horse and Shee-kee for five or six years before returning to Shepaconah's village on the banks of the Mississinewa.

As Shepoconah's dutiful wife, Maconaquah not only looked Indian, but thought and spoke in the traditional Indian way. Out in the western wilderness, she forgot the few remaining English names or words she had once known. She stopped worrying that she would be found and made to return to the white man's world. With Shepoconah and his people, she believed she was finally safe at home.

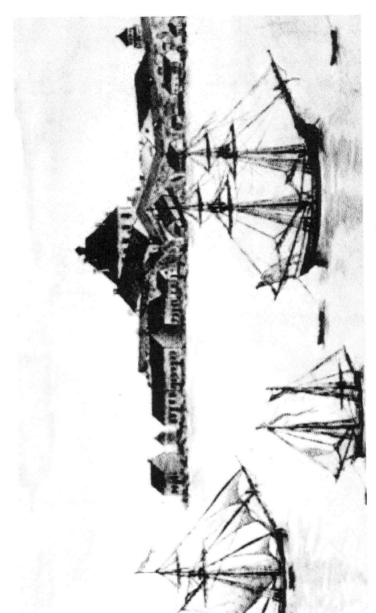

Old fort Niagara by an unknown artist
courtesy of the Old fort Niagara Association

CHAPTER III

THE SEARCH FOR FRANCES

Ruth Slocum never lost hope that Frances was alive and would be found. Frances was nearly six years old when she was taken. Surely she would always remember her family name and where they lived. Perhaps she would escape from her Indian captors and make her way to white people who would befriend her. Ruth's faith in this was so strong that she wouldn't leave the Wyoming homestead even after another tragedy.

On the 16th of December, just six weeks after Frances and Wareham had been abducted, Jonathan and his father-in-law, Isaac Tripp, were shot and killed by Indians as they were feeding their cattle. William was shot in one of his feet as he ran to Fort Wyoming to alarm the militia. As before, the Indians escaped. They knew about hidden caves and trails. With their deerskin moccasins they could walk long distances in cold weather, leaving no trail.

Giles was now head of the household, and the family feared the Indians might return to kill him.

"I'm not afraid, Mother," Giles assured Ruth. "Thee and Father told us the Lord would take care of those who help themselves. Thee wouldn't want the Lord - or the Indians - to think we were afraid by running from trouble. Surely peace will come some day. This land is too good to leave. I think Father and Grandfather would want us to stay."

"Thee is right, Giles," William added. "Together we can do the chores around here. I just know we can."

Ebenezer wasn't to be left out. "Father always said I'm good in the shop, makin' and repairin' things. I can do that for thee, Mother." Smiling at eight-year-old Benjamin, Ebenezer added, "I'll let thee be my helper."

Eighteen-year-old Judith and ten-year-old Mary had been sharing the household chores with their mother since the birth of Jonathan in September. Between caring for the new baby and two-year-old Joseph, they were as skilled at child care as they were adept in cooking, spinning, sewing, and the many other tasks in a pioneer household which were needed for survival.

The sorrowing family knew they had the strength to stay in spite of their devastating losses. As for Frances, if she couldn't make her way back to them, they would begin searching again as soon as they were able. Even though the Revolutionary War ended in 1781, it wasn't safe to travel for some time afterwards. When word came to the valley that the Treaty of Paris had been signed in 1783, the Slocums decided the time had come to resume the search for Frances.

"I've heard there is an important British fort and Indian village north of the Great Falls of the Niagara River. I think we should start there," Giles said after looking at the positions of the various Indian tribes and British strongholds. "If the Indians that raided here in 1778 were from the north, that settlement would have been their headquarters. Frances could have been taken there. Maybe she's still there!"

Ruth was encouraged. "Perhaps offering a reward of money would help," she suggested. "Do take some along. Surely someone there will remember a white girl with lovely red hair."

In 1784, Giles and William went north to Fort Niagara, offering a reward of 100 guineas for information about their sister. They spent two weeks talking with Indian traders, French trappers, soldiers and tradesmen, spreading the word of their inquiry and reward money. They took interpreters with them to the Indian village where they spent many days questioning members of the tribes still encamped there. During their long evenings, the brothers talked about their plight by the flickering light of their campfire.

"I just don't understand it, Giles," William said. "I can tell they're lying. That last fella today wouldn't even look us in the face. He knew who we were talking about. Why won't they talk?"

"It's hard to understand, William," Giles agreed. "Even though they can use the money, they say they never heard of such a person. There must be some sort of code up here, or maybe they're afraid to talk. It's plain to see we're wasting our time here. I think it's best to move on while we still have our hides and the money. It won't do Mother and the others any good if we get ourselves killed trying to find Frances."

If they had only thought to check the government records, they would have seen the names of the Tory families sent to Canada four years earlier - including the mention of the "Hookam and Kingsley" children. Other names on that list would have been helpful clues in discovering with whom she was living.

Four years later, in 1788, the brothers spent several months inquiring about Frances among the settlements and Indian villages in the wilderness of the Ohio country. This time they offered a reward of $500, but again, nobody would talk.

Word came to the Slocums in 1789 of an exchange of prisoners taken by the Indians during the war. Ruth made the trip to Tioga Point (now Athens, Pennsylvania) hoping to either find Frances or learn of her whereabouts. She spent many weeks speaking with the released prisoners, but none of them were able to help her. She, too, returned home bitterly disappointed.

At about that time, Frances' cousin, Isaac Tripp, returned to the Wyoming Valley. His report to the Slocums that he had seen Frances at the Indian encampment by Fort Niagara and that she had been well cared for by her Indian captors inspired the family to renew their efforts to find her.

In November of 1790, William returned to Tioga Point, where the United States Commissioner, Colonel Timothy Pickering, was conducting a council with the Chiefs of the Seneca Indian tribes. Many chiefs of other tribes within the Six Nations Confederation also attended to air their grievances with the government. William had a chance to talk with many of them, and somehow William got the idea that Frances was living among the Mohawk Indians.

He told Col. Pickering of this and complained that his sister had not been released as yet. The Colonel issued a document to the members of the Six Nations demanding that their prisoner, Frances Slocum, be immediately released to

Joseph Smith, an interpreter at the council. In reality, this meant nothing since Frances had never lived with the Mohawks or any member of the Six Nations, but it gave the Slocums hope for some time.

In the spring of 1791, Giles set out to explore Chief Cornplanter's territory at the headwaters of the Allegheny River. At Tioga Point he joined Colonel Thomas Proctor's party of men who were on their way to visit the Indian tribes living along the Wabash River. They had been commissioned by the government to establish peace and friendly relations with the Indians of that area and around the Great Lakes. Giles asked the Colonel to be on the lookout for his sister, a red-haired woman of eighteen years.

A month later, Col. Proctor made an entry in his journal while at Buffalo Creek (now Buffalo, New York) of a payment he made to a white prisoner, Francis Slocum. The background story he related did not match that of Frances, and it was unlikely she would have traveled so far from Kekionga. Proctor's cryptic entry remains another unsolved mystery.

In July of the same year, William again attended a treaty held at Newtown (Elmira, New York) with Col. Pickering and the chiefs of the Six Nations. Neither the Colonel nor the interpreter, Joseph Smith, had heard news of Frances being held by any of the tribes represented.

Because of the fierce conflicts raging between Indians and the citizens of the new United States of America, the Slocums had to postpone their search for six years. Early in the autumn of 1797, Giles, William, Benjamin, and Isaac started out with a drove of cattle and a quantity of dry goods to give their long journey the appearance of a business trip.

At Seneca Lake, and again at Lake Erie, the brothers separated. The dry goods were loaded on a boat which stopped at all towns on one side of the lakes, where inquiries about Frances were made while the goods were offered for sale. Isaac herded the cattle overland along the northern side of Lake Erie, which carried him through British-controlled villages and Indian encampments. He made inquiries everywhere he passed. By the time he met his brothers in Detroit, Isaac had worn out his shoes, and much of his clothing, and was nearly starved.

The Slocum brothers contacted white traders in Detroit, offering $300 to any who would bring Frances to them. The traders told them frankly, that they would never reveal knowledge of an Indian captive, because they wouldn't live long if they did. The frontier code was more powerful than reward money.

While Frances, who had become Maconaquah, was living near Kekionga with her husband, Shepoconah, her brothers organized their last hunt for the little sister who had been stolen from them so many years ago. In 1798 they looked among the northern and western Indians, but didn't go far enough west. If they had, they might have found her.

The Slocum family's efforts to find Frances had become almost legendary on the frontier. One day, a woman appeared at the family home in Wilkes-Barre, hoping she might be the missing Frances. She had been taken captive so young that she could not remember her birth name. Ruth knew immediately that she was not her missing daughter, but invited the woman to stay with them. After staying with the Slocums for a few months, the woman left to continue the search for her own family.

By 1800, all of the Slocum children were grown and married. Most had moved on to live in other places. Only Joseph, William, and Jonathan lived near their mother in Wilkes-Barre, which had grown to a busy town of nearly one thousand people. The three brothers farmed enough land to supply their food. Joseph was also a successful blacksmith and a member of the local militia known as the Wyoming Blues. William still carried the rifle ball in his leg from the Indian attack that killed his father and grandfather, but he was well able to serve three years as Sheriff of Luzerne County. Judith, married to Hugh Forseman, lived in nearby Sheshequin, Pennsylvania. Giles established his family in Saratoga County, New York, and Mary resided in Circleville, Ohio, with her husband, Joseph Towne. Ebenezer, a Captain in the Wyoming Blues, bought land north of Wilkes-Barre which was called "Capouse," "Roaring Brook," and "Deep Hollow" (now Scranton, Pennsylvania). Benjamin joined Ebenezer there in operating a grist mill, a sawmill, a distillery, and a blacksmith shop with a two-fire forge.

With their own families to care for, the brothers no longer had time to search for their sister. It was hard to believe that Frances had been missing for twenty-two years. The little girl who had been taken from them would have been twenty-seven years old. Ruth, with the instinct of a mother, stubbornly refused to consider that Frances might be dead. She pleaded with her sons to search again for her long-lost daughter. Joseph tried to reason with her.

"It appears to us that if Frances were still alive, she would have made herself known to white people by now. There just isn't a spot any more that isn't touched by white families, either moving in or passing by on their way out west. We've all heard of the many captives released that go right back to their Indian tribes. They must think that easy way of life is better than ours somehow. Maybe she doesn't want to be found, Mother. Probably Frances is happy wherever she is."

Ruth would not be put off. "I just want to see her again. I want to beg her forgiveness for letting the Indians carry her off. Oh, how she must have wondered why I asked them to let Ebenezer go and not her! Perhaps she hates me for that. I must explain. I just want to see her. Oh why didn't I follow them into the woods that day?"

"Don't fret so, Mother," Joseph said, trying to comfort her. "We'd like to find her, too, but a better way to hunt nowadays is by letters to government officials. So many tribes are migrating across the Mississippi, it'd be near impossible to visit them all. Besides, that way of finding her proved futile these past sixteen years. We'll contact everyone concerned with Indians - and pray for a miracle."

When they had children of their own, Ruth's sons and daughters better understood their mother's torment. Ruth died seven years later, still obsessed with the vision of barefooted little Frances being carried off into the woods over the shoulder of an Indian. The remaining children promised their dying mother they would never stop looking for Frances. They would seek out and follow any leads.

Nineteen years passed before the next lead presented itself. Isaac was living in Bellevue, Ohio, when he heard that a Wyandot chief in nearby Upper Sandusky had a white wife. Joseph traveled from his home in Wilkes-Barre to join Isaac in visiting this family.

They felt sure they would be able to identify her. When Frances was still a toddler, one of her brothers had accidentally hit the end of her left forefinger so hard that it was permanently disfigured. No matter how much Frances had changed in forty-eight years, they would always recognize that finger with its nail which could not grow back. They were disappointed once again. The Wyandot wife did not have a disfigured left forefinger.

Giles died in November of 1826. The few remaining members of Frances' immediate family were getting old and living in scattered locations. They had resigned themselves to never seeing Frances again, but their grandchildren never tired of hearing the stories of pioneer days. Their favorite was the mystery of Great Aunt Frances and of the many trips into Indian lands to find her. She had become a family legend, told and retold many times.

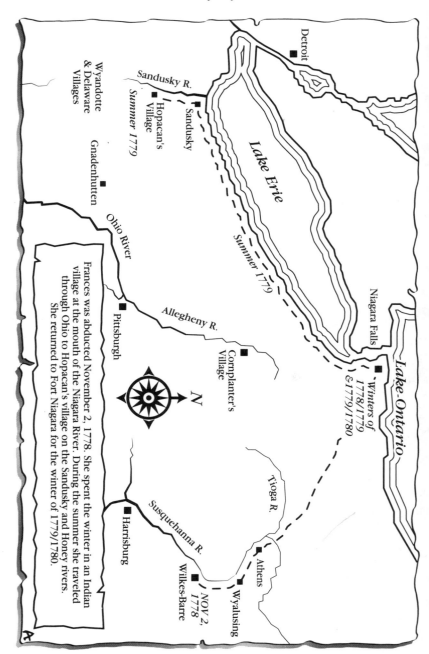

Detroit

Sandusky R.

Wyandotte
& Delaware
Villages

Hopacan's
Village

Summer 1779

Sandusky

Lake Erie

Gnadenhutten

Ohio River

Summer 1779

Niagara Falls

Lake Ontario

*Winters of
1778/1779
& 1779/1780*

Allegheny R.

Pittsburgh

Cornplanter's
Village

N

Tioga R.

Athens

Wyalusing

*NOV 2,
1778*

Susquehanna R.

Wilkes-Barre

Harrisburg

Frances was abducted November 2, 1778. She spent the winter in an Indian village at the mouth of the Niagara River. During the summer she traveled through Ohio to Hopacan's village on the Sandusky and Honey rivers. She returned to Fort Niagara for the winter of 1779/1780.

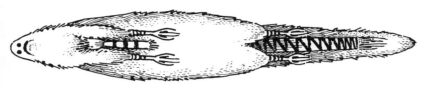

CHAPTER IV

A MIRACLE HAPPENS

Maconaquah, who had once been She-let-a-wash, and before that Frances Slocum, was content to remain with her husband, Shepoconah, in his village on the Mississinewa River, about seven miles upstream from where it empties into the Wabash River in the state of Indiana. Frances' smashed finger was such a curiosity to the Miamis that Maconaquah and Shepoconah named their first-born daughter Ke-ke-na-kush-wa, meaning "Cut Finger" in the Miami tongue. Sadly, as remote as they sometimes seemed to be from the clashes of the world beyond, their lives there were not destined to be peaceful ones.

After the American Army chased the British back to Canada in the War of 1812, the government forces took on the Indian tribes still living north of the Ohio River. They wanted the Indian land for the ever-increasing number of settlers coming west. The Miamis knew they needed strong, firm leadership to deal with the whites in treaty negotiations, but Shepocohah was becoming too deaf to be the leader they needed. He was soon replaced by two men, Francis Godfroy as War Chief and Jean Baptiste Richardville, Civil Chief.

Shepoconah and Maconaquah moved several miles further upstream and established what became known as the

Deaf Man's Village at the site of a good spring. Three more children were born to them. Their two sons died but another daughter, whom they named O-zah-shin-quah, or "Yellow Leaf," survived. She was about ten years younger than her sister, Ke-ke-na-kush-wa.

The Treaty of 1818, defining the boundaries of Indian land in Indiana, sharply curtailed the Indians' ability to hunt for meat for their families, and it became necessary to raise cattle, hogs, chickens, and geese to supplement what they could grow. Some Miamis didn't approve of those who were adopting white man's ways. They thought it best to sell their remaining land and move farther west where they could live in the traditional Indian way. This argument raged on for over twenty years, greatly dividing the Miamis. Their lands were whittled down even more with the Treaty of 1826, when the Indians sold their lands north and west of the Wabash and Miami (Maumee) Rivers, along with additional land, for the Wabash and Erie Canal.

During those treaty years, Maconaquah's family had grown up. The name of Ke-ke-na-kush-wa's first husband, or what happened to him is unknown, but that marriage gave Maconaquah her first granddaughter. Ke-ke-na-kush-wa's second marriage was to Captain Jean Baptiste Brouillette, whose father was a Frenchman. He used his French name, but was raised by his Indian mother and always lived as an Indian.

O-zah-shin-quah's first husband was Louis Godfroy, Chief Frances Godfroy's nephew, by whom she had two daughters. It is said that Louis abused his wife so was either killed or thrown out of the family. Her second marriage was to Wap-shing-qah. They also had a daughter before he met a violent death.

Shepoconah died in 1833. A sorrowful Maconaquah buried him by the graves of their sons and raised a pole with a white flag at the top so the Great Spirit would know where to find him. Although she promised Shepoconah she wouldn't leave their land, she secretly wondered how long the Miamis could hold out against the dreaded whites who were moving in so quickly. The Indian lands grew smaller as the white towns and farms grew larger. Already many Indian tribes had moved to new lands to the west. It was only a matter of time before the Miamis, too, would be crowded out.

Surely, Maconaquah thought, the Great White Father would not make her move to another place. She was the wife of a great chief. But Maconaquah was getting old and was no longer certain of a great many things. She only knew that when she died, she must be buried by Shepoconah and their sons. This was necessary so she could be with them in the Spirit Land.

She decided to appeal to the Great Spirit for guidance and help, but before Great Spirit would look favorably upon her, Maconaquah knew, she must unburden her mind of the secret she had carried for so many years. It bothered her a lot lately, this fear that maybe Great Spirit did not wish her to take such a burden with her into death.

Her beloved adopted people had always warned her, "If your white family finds you, they will make you return to them." She never wished to live with white people, or be like them in any way, so she had remained silent and made no attempt to contact her white family. Now the idea that Great Spirit did not approve of her decision had gotten into her head and just wouldn't leave. At long last, she would have to tell. But how?

One cold winter day, in January of 1835, a white trader by the name of George Ewing stopped at Maconaquah's cabin seeking food and shelter for the night. He was always a welcome and trusted visitor. Ewing had lived along the area's rivers for so long, he knew the ways of the Indians and spoke in their tongue. He always brought news with him, and sometimes silver ornaments for the wives to sew onto their clothing or hair pieces.

It was the custom for Indians to retire for the night shortly after supper, but this night Maconaquah hesitated. "I have something on my mind," she told Ewing. "I am old and weak. I shan't live long and I must tell it. I can't die in peace if I don't." Slowly she pushed her sleeve back from her weatherbeaten hand and lower arm and displayed the white skin above her elbow.

With Ewing's encouragement, Maconaquah haltingly told him what she could remember about her life before she had been abducted. She remembered a house near a fort and the Susquehanna River. There had been a man named Slocum - her father - who had always worn a big, black hat. She described the Indian raid when she and a boy were taken, and Ewing had the eerie feeling that he was listening to the little girl she had once been. Her voice grew stronger as she talked of her life as an Indian and how good it had been.

Much relieved, Maconaquah exclaimed, "There! Now I can die! You don't know how much this has troubled me, friend." Her old face wore a peaceful look. The Great Spirit was pleased with her. She could feel it.

Ewing thought about Maconaquah as he rode back to his home in Logansport the next day. There seemed to be a lot of interest these days in other captives who had been found after many years, but he had never imagined that he would find himself part of such a story as it unfolded. He guessed Maconaquah to be about seventy. How incredible, he thought to himself. She must have been taken before the War for Independence more than fifty years ago! Her family must have given her up for dead years ago.

By the time Ewing reached home, he knew he would make an attempt to locate Maconaquah's white family. It was possible that some of them were still alive. But how could he go about contacting them? He knew the Susquehanna River was in the eastern part of Pennsylvania and thought that the city of Lancaster was an old town in that general vicinity. Surely the postmaster there would know if there was a Slocum family in the area, and certainly he could make the story known. Ewing assembled paper, ink, and pen and carefully wrote:

...her own Christian name she has forgotten, but says her father's name was something like Slocum, and he was a Quaker. She also recollects that it was upon the Susquehanna River that they lived, but doesn't recollect the name of the town near where they lived. I have thought from this letter you might cause something to be inserted in the newspapers of your country that might possibly catch the eye of some of the descendants of the Slocum family, who have knowledge of a girl having been carried off by Indians some seventy years ago. This they might know from family traditions. If so, and they will come here, I will carry them where they may see the object of my letter, alive and happy, though old and far advanced in life...

The postmistress at Lancaster, Pennsylvania, was Mary Dickson, who was also the editor of the local newspaper, The Intelligencer. For reasons known only to herself, she never published Ewing's letter. Perhaps she thought it unimportant, or more likely, she simply mislaid it. For two years the letter lay somewhere, ignored by everyone, until the miracle for which the Slocums had prayed for half a century finally happened. Someone found the letter and brought it to the attention of the new editor, John W. Forney.

Forney was greatly interested and published the letter in its entirety in July of 1837, within a special edition of the paper with a wider circulation than usual because of its temperance notices. It was an edition all area clergymen were sure to see. Forney also wrote an editorial on the matter entitled, "Important Disclosure." He stated that he could not imagine why it had taken the letter so long to get the attention it deserved. He hoped someone who knew of a Slocum family in the area would notify the newspaper. Though the Indian captive might have already died, Forney thought it important to try to contact any family members if they could be found.

The Reverend Samuel Bowman, formerly of Wilkes-Barre, received his copy of the special edition and read the letter with great interest. He knew the story of the Indian raids in the Wyoming Valley during the Revolutionary War and of the tragedies of the Slocum family. He even knew that Joseph Slocum still lived in the handsome, three-story brick house on the square in Wilkes-Barre. Bowman immediately forwarded his copy of The Intelligencer to him.

Joseph tried not to get too excited. He had been disappointed too many times before, and even if it was Frances, she might be dead. After all, it had been two years since the trader way out in Indiana had written his letter. Ewing himself might have moved on, as traders had a way of doing. So many ifs! Nevertheless, he would follow up the lead as he had all the others. He had promised his mother he would never stop trying.

Joseph wrote Mary and Isaac of this new possibility while his son, Jonathan, who was a lawyer, answered Ewing's letter on August 8, 1837:

"...we have received, but a few days ago, a letter written by you to a gentleman in Lancaster, of this state, upon a subject of deep and intense interest to our family. How the matter could have lain so long wrapped in obscurity we cannot conceive. An aunt of mine, sister of my father, was taken away when five years old, by the Indians, and since then we have only had vague and indistinct rumors upon the subject. Your letter we deem to have entirely revealed the whole matter, and set everything at rest. The description is so perfect, and the incidents (with the exception of her age) so correct, that we feel confident.

Steps will be taken immediately to investigate the matter, and we will endeavor to do all in our power to restore a lost relative who has been sixty years in Indian bondage..."

George Ewing had not moved on. He also happened to be at home when Jonathan's letter arrived and was astonished to finally receive an answer. Long ago he had decided that Maconaquah's immediate family must all be deceased and the present generation uninterested in her story. On August 26, 1837, Ewing answered:

Dear Sir: I have the pleasure of acknowledging receipt of your letter of the 8th instant, and in answer can add, that the female I spoke of in January, 1835, is still alive; nor can I for a moment doubt but that she is the identical relative that has been so long lost to your family...

Ewing also described Maconaquah as a highly respected woman, but with manners, customs, and speech entirely Indian. He suggested that if they arrived to visit her while he, Ewing, was away, they should contact James Miller of nearby Peru, who would accompany them to act as interpreter. Miller worked in the Ewing store in Peru and was fluent in the Miami language. Peru also would be the closest town to Deaf Man's Village at which the Slocum's could find accommodations.

The whole town of Wilkes-Barre was in a frenzy of excitement after Joseph received Ewing's most recent letter. The Indian woman living in Deaf Man's Village on the banks of the Mississinewa River in Indiana was really, truly Frances Slocum - and she was still alive! Perhaps Joseph would bring her back to Wilkes-Barre so they could see for themselves this living legend of the early days, when the town was just a fort watching over the settlers.

Joseph quickly wrote Isaac and Mary with the wonderful

news and plans for the reunion with Frances. Accompanied by Isaac, he would come to Circleville and pick up Mary for the trip to Indiana. The wait for Joseph and a detour to Circleville seemed an intolerable delay to Isaac, who lived much closer to Peru. He had searched too long and too often to waste another day. With the Wabash and Erie Canal so close to his home in Bellevue, he could reach Deaf Man's Village in a week's time. After nearly sixty years, he would be with Frances by next week! He packed his bags and left immediately.

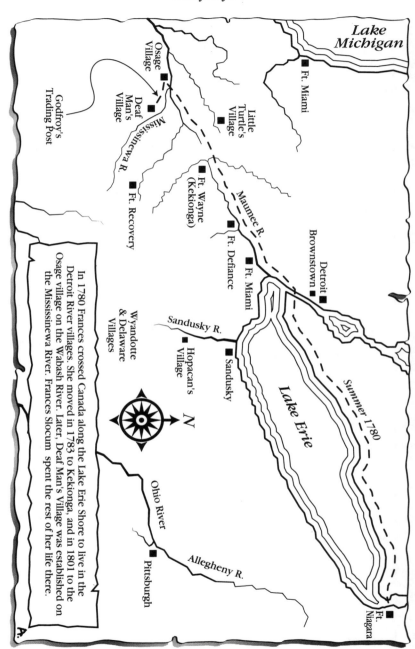

In 1780 Frances crossed Canada along the Lake Erie Shore to live in the Detroit River villages. She moved in 1783 to Kekionga, and in 1801 to the Osage village on the Wabash River. Later, Deaf Man's Village was established on the Mississinewa River. Frances Slocum spent the rest of her life there.

CHAPTER V

MACONAQUAH PLEASES THE GREAT SPIRIT

Maconaquah watched apprehensively as two riders splashed across the river to her cabin. She recognized James Miller, but who was the other? What business could they have with her? Whites were almost always trouble. They were moving into Indian lands in great numbers, stealing her ponies and cattle. They acted like the land was theirs and the Indians were unwelcome trespassers. It was all wrong, backwards, but what could she do? What could anybody do? They were like a great tornado, tearing up everything in their path.

When she had come to this bountiful land as Shepoconah's wife, the land had been free for everyone to use. The Indians were happy, tending the crops in the summer and hunting for game in the winter. That life was gone now, since the white people had come, building their forts, bringing only firewater and sickness to the Indians. Her grandchildren, Maconaquah feared, would never know how good the life had been, or the joy of living in the traditional way.

Suspiciously, Maconaquah watched the riders dismount and approach her cabin. They seemed so happy. If these white people were so happy, it must mean more trouble for the Indians. This visit could not be good news.

Miller greeted her courteously as she stepped outside to meet them, then introduced the other man as her blood brother who had come a great distance to find her. This brother, this Isaac, knew about her damaged finger. He kept pointing to it and smiling while tears filled his eyes.

Maconaquah listened passively as Miller interpreted this strange brother's words, which rushed from his mouth so quickly he seemed breathless. There was much about her abduction as a child and the many efforts of her brothers to find her.

This was not what she had wanted! She had only meant to make her peace with Great Spirit before dying. Instead, telling her secret had brought her more trouble! She listened quietly, while watching and listening for signs of trickery. She knew this man, who said he was her brother, would try to make her leave her home and live in the hated white man's world.

She became aware that Miller was speaking to her directly. He was telling her that another brother and a sister were on their way to see her. They had farther to travel but would come to visit as soon as they arrived in Peru. More trouble!

Frances' lack of response to their reunion hurt Isaac deeply. He had thought she would be delighted to see him again, but instead, she had seemed cold and distant. He couldn't understand it at all. He comforted himself by hoping that Mary and Joseph might have better luck.

Mary and Joseph were sure, too, they would have better luck. As soon as they were established at the Bearss Hotel in Peru, they set out with Isaac and James Miller, the interpreter, for Deaf Man's Village.

The Slocum party first stopped at Mount Pleasant, Chief Francis Godfroy's trading post where, according to Indian protocol, Miller introduced them to the Chief and told him of their mission. Chief Godfroy was over six feet tall and weighed some three hundred pounds. He wore a long, ruffled calico shirt which came nearly to his leggings, and his long hair was tied at the back of his neck. He appeared very solemn and majestic as he wished them well and offered his assistance if it was needed.

Mary was confident that Frances would be happy to see the older sister who'd cared for her from the time she was a baby. They'd had so many good times together. And now, after nearly sixty years they would be together again! Her spirits soared as their party rode along the trail in the golden glow of an autumn day.

Joseph was surprised and impressed by his first look at Frances' home. The main house consisted of two larger cabins connected by a smaller one, perhaps used as a covered walkway. Smaller outbuildings for tools and equipment and a neat little spring house lay beyond. Chickens, geese, and hogs roamed freely, while ponies and cattle grazed in a nearby pasture. The place was obviously prosperous and well cared for. Dismounting, the party entered a tidy yard enclosed by a rail fence and approached the cabin.

Maconaquah admitted them to her cabin begrudgingly and immediately seated herself, facing her visitors, as if ready for interrogation. Her two daughters, son-in-law Captain Brouillette, and the grandchildren hovered protectively behind her. James Miller solemnly made the introductions, using Frances' Indian name, Mary sadly noted.

Maconaquah listened, passively, while her white family told of the many searches they had made for her, of the great sums of money offered for her rescue, and how their mother had never lost faith that she was alive somewhere and would be reunited with her family.

How strange, Mary thought despairingly, that we are telling this old Indian woman of our desperate search for a little red-haired girl we never stopped loving - and they are one and the same. If only there was a way to connect the Frances who was with the Frances who is!

"Do you remember your given name?" Mary asked suddenly.

Maconaquah said stiffly, "It is a long time. I do not know."

"Was it Frances?" Mary asked gently.

Some memory moved in Maconaquah's old eyes when she heard the name. "Yes - Franca. Franca!" Her mouth wanted to smile as it produced the alien sound, but she recovered her composure in time resuming her stoic expression.

Isaac regretted that he hadn't warned Mary and Joseph beforehand of Frances' cold behavior. He could see they were as upset as he had been the first time he had tried to speak with her. He suggested they step outside for a breath of air.

"She doesn't seem to feel any kinship with us at all," Joseph said sadly. "Is there no way to win Frances' trust?"

"Did you bring any gifts for your Indian family?" Miller asked suddenly.

"No," Joseph replied. I guess we were so excited about finally finding her that we never thought of it." He gazed off toward the pasture. "It never occurred to us that a gift would be necessary in order to be welcomed. This is all very strange behavior."

"What kind of a gift could we get way out here?" Mary asked.

"Maybe we could invite them to supper," Isaac said suddenly. "The people at the Bearss Hotel are very interested in our mission and they've offered to help in whatever way they can."

"A gift of food is always welcome to Indians," Miller said. "It just might work."

Returning to the cabin in better spirits, they found Frances seated on the floor, scraping a deerskin. She ignored them.

Mary felt her joints creak as she sat down on the floor, facing Frances. Did Frances' do this all the time? Aloud, she said, "Frances - Maconaquah - will you and your family please join me and our brothers for supper back at the hotel in Peru? We would be honored to have you as our guests."

Maconaquah's hands slowly stopped their scraping as Miller interpreted Mary's words. They were offering a gift - a sign of friendship. She pondered this offer, looking for tricks, but decided that if her daughters and Brouillette accompanied her, she couldn't be taken away. She would be safe. Still, it would be better to talk this over with Chief Godfroy.

While members of both her families waited, Maconaquah splashed across the river to Mt. Pleasant on her pony and returned a short time later to accept her white family's invitation. Her daughters were obviously pleased with her decision, although in deference to their mother, they tried not to show it. Perhaps during the gift dinner they would be able to satisfy their own curiosities.

After further delay, the party rode single file, Indian style, along the ten-mile trail to Peru. Maconaquah maintained her silence until the large party had been received and made comfortable at Bearss Hotel. Speaking in low tones to Miller, she gestured to her daughter, Ke-ke-na-kush-wa, to place an object wrapped in a white cloth upon a table. Miller turned to the Slocums and explained that Maconaquah wished to make a presentation.

"Gift-givin' is important to the Indians," he said. "They make quite a ceremony of it. No matter what it is, take it serious and show your gratitude in a serious way."

Maconaquah began to speak again, and Miller interpreted her words as meaning that she and her Indian family desired friendship with the members of her white family who had journeyed so far to meet her. They offered a gift to seal that friendship.

Isaac, Joseph, and Mary looked at each other wordlessly, seeing the hope in each other's eyes. "Why don't you speak for us, Mary," Isaac said. "She does seem to respond to you."

Mary stepped forward with the same solemn dignity Ke-ke-na-kush-wa had shown, and removed the white cloth to reveal a large venison quarter. Mary had not forgotten the harsh realities of frontier life. Such a large gift of food from people whose survival depended on what they could hunt and grow was deeply meaningful.

She raised her eyes and looked directly at Maconaquah.

"We are honored to accept such a generous gift from our sister and her family," she said, trying not to cry, "And we are honored by the gift of their friendship."

When Miller had finished interpreting Mary's words, Maconaquah smiled. Everyone was smiling when they sat down to the Slocum's gift of supper.

After they were finished, Maconaquah told her relatives they had to return to their village but would return the next day to talk more. Although the next day was Sunday, many citizens of Peru did not attend church services. Like the Slocums, they waited for the return of Maconaquah and her family, as she had promised the night before. The townspeople were familiar with the sight of the old Indian woman riding her pony into town, but everyone wanted a closer look, now that they'd learned she was really a white woman whose family was obviously wealthy. They had read stories of other former captives in the popular press and wanted the opportunity to witness such a drama firsthand. People crowded around the hotel, waiting and talking among themselves in an excited buzz.

Within, the Slocums also waited. They were uncomfortable about not properly observing the Sabbath and struggled to understand that Frances would have forgotten such things long ago. After all, she had been a five-year-old child, far from churches and ministers and the teachings of her own dear mother. It was only natural that she would have forgotten. But would she remember that she had promised to return today and talk with them some more?

Outside, the noise of the crowd increased, and presently Maconaquah and her family entered, regally attired in colorful clothing, richly decorated with silk applique, ribbons, beading and silver broaches.

With more time to prepare, the proprietors of the Bearss Hotel provided the very best of food and accommodations for the historic event. After a sumptuous breakfast, which did not appear to be to the Indian's taste, the family retired for a visit in private.

"I never tired of living with the Indians," Maconaquah said. "I always had enough to live on and have lived well." She paused and then said something to Miller in a low, angry voice.

"Maconaquah wonders why you don't look at her while she speaks," he said to Mary as she dipped a pen into ink and then scribbled another word on the paper before her.

Mary looked up, flustered. "Please tell Maconaquah that I am setting down her words so that they may be remembered exactly. Other members of our family back East will want to know what she said and I want to be sure I don't forget a thing."

Miller and Maconaquah spoke in low tones for some minutes. Finally she nodded her head in Mary's direction, as if giving permission.

"Maconaquah is uncomfortable with the idea of her words being saved like dried corn," Miller said. "But she understands that white people don't know how to carry words in their heads as the Indians do. She will allow you to gather her words on the paper."

"Thank her for me," Mary said gravely, fighting the urge to smile.

While still in Peru for this dramatic reunion, Mary did send a detailed letter back to Wilkes-Barre, which was

*published in its entirety in the <u>Wyoming Republican</u>
newspaper.*

Maconaquah resumed her story. "I never heard of my
white family's search for me. I never thought anything of
them unless it was for a little while after I was taken."

She related what she remembered of her abduction and
the flight to Tuck Horse's village. She told them of her life
with her adopted family, of her marriages and children, and
of life on the banks of the Mississinewa River.

Maconaquah's straightforward statement that she had
thought little of her family after her abduction caused the
Slocum's sadness when they remembered the years of worry
and fruitless searching. Although it was difficult for the
Slocums to understand how their Frances could have
forgotten her life with them, and, seemingly, so willingly
adapted to life as an Indian, they couldn't help but notice
how happy a life it had been for her. It had obviously been
a good life and, for that, they were grateful. If only their
mother could have known.

Joseph told his Indian sister, "I live where our father and
mother used to live, by the beautiful Susquehanna. We want
you to return with us, and we will give you of our property
and you shall be one of us, sharing all that we have. You
shall have a good house and everything you desire. Oh, do
go back with us!"

Maconaquah was very moved by her brother's
generosity, so she answered gently. "No, I cannot. I have
always lived with the Indians, and they have always used me
very kindly. I am used to them. The Great Spirit has always
allowed me to live with them and I wish to live and die with

them. Why should I go and be like a fish out of water?"

"But won't you at least go and make a visit to your early home, and then when you have seen it, return again to your grandchildren?" Joseph persisted.

"I cannot, I cannot," Maconaquah answered sadly. "I am an old tree and cannot move about. I am afraid I should die and never come back. I shall die here and lie in that graveyard, and they will raise the pole at my grave with the white flag on it, and the Great Spirit will know where to find me. I should not be happy with my white relatives. I am glad enough to see them, but I cannot go with them. I cannot."

She gestured firmly. "I have done."

Though Maconaquah's refusal was disappointing, the Slocums realized that all Frances had said was true. Maconaquah would be "like a fish out of water" in the world of the white man, an object of curiosity wherever she went. None of them wished that for her.

They stopped urging Frances to return home with them and settled down to enjoy their days with her and her family. They were comforted by the fact that they would be able to visit often now that the canals reached far into the frontier. For her part, Maconaquah realized it was her white relatives who had brought happiness again to Deaf Man's Village. There was love and laughter as two parts of the same family tried to understand each other's language and ways.

"A Silver Cross"
Maconaquah's cross given to her by her parents
when she was a young girl

George Winter's description of Kick-ke-se-quah:

"Kick-ke-se-quah, Brouillette's wife, was a fine tall and graceful woman, with an exceptional face, sharp piercing eyes that indicated a capacity to penetrate below the surface of things. She was very gracious towards me; and I could but feel that they regarded me as a friend of Joseph Slocum."

Kick-ke-se-quah by George Winter
Tippecanoe County Historical Association, Lafayette, Indiana.
Gift of Mrs. Cable G. Ball

George Winter's description of Bourillette:

*"I remember very distinctly when I first saw Brouillette.
He was on a visit to Logansport in the fall of the year of the
'payment'...*

*The 'sketch (of Brouillette)...I made in 1837, when
attending the last Pottawattamie payment made east of the
Mississippi River...at Demoss's House Michigan Road.*

*He was a 'French half breed' of elegant appearance,
very straight and slim. In personal appearance he had a
decided commanding mien. In height he stood six feet two
inches. His tout en semble was unique, as his aboriginal
costume was expensively shewy. He wore around his head
a rich figured crimson shawl a la turban, with long flowing
ends gracefully falling over the shoulders. Silver ornaments
- or clusters of earbobs testified their weight by a partial
elongation of the ears.*

*He wore a fine frock of the latest fashion. (When the
Indian assumes the white man's garb, he always chooses a
frock coat. It is an object of beauty to his eye.) His 'pes-
mo-kin', or shirt was white, spotted with a small red figure,
overhanging very handsome blue leggings..."*

Bouriette by George Winter
Tippecanoe County Historical Association, Lafayette, Indiana.
Gift of Mrs. Cable G. Ball

George Winter's description of Frances Godfrey - War Chief:

"Personally Chief Frances Godfroy was a very remarkable fine looking man. His tout en semble would attract the attention of the observer were he among a large congregated number of indians. He was fully six feet in height, remarkably portly - his avoirdupois being perhaps some 350 pounds.

His eye was larger than that of the general characteristic eye of the indian which is rather small, sharp and piercing. Godfroy's nose was bulby and wide-spreading and in no way characteristic on the Miami type which is more of aquiline form. His lips were large and somewhat pouting. His hair was disposed to have curly tendencies.

When I knew him in the year 1838 - he visited my studio in Logansport - his hair was tinged with autumnal frost which gave him a dignified and more impressive appearance.

He wore a queque, which is common among the aborigines of the Wabash, with wide black ribbon bow attached, with long ends falling over and following the curved line of his broad and massive back, which gave him a caste of the 'gentleman of the old school' character."

Frances Godfroy - War Chief by George Winter
Tippecanoe County Historical Association, Lafayette, Indiana.
Gift of Mrs. Cable G. Ball

George Winter's description of the 'Three Women', Frances Slocum and her daughters Kick-ke-se-quah and O-shaw-se-quah:

"Frances looked upon her likeness with complacency, Kick-ke-se-quah eyed it approvingly, yet suspiciously - it was a mystery. The widowed daughter, O-shaw-se-quah, would not look at it, but turned away from it abruptly when I presented it to her for her inspection, as though some evil surrounded it."

The Three Women by George Winter
Tippecanoe County Historical Association, Lafayette, Indiana.
Gift of Mrs. Cable G. Ball

CHAPTER VI

KINSHIP WORKS ITS MAGIC

James Miller liked spring for the usual reasons. The days were longer and the warmth of the sun felt good. He especially liked riding through the woods with its rich smell of rotting leaves. It inspired him to think that out of the debris of past years would spring new life to feed the future. Miller felt like singing at the top of his voice. He laughed aloud. Imagine what the Indians would think if they caught him singing through the forest! They would scowl at him more than usual.

He laughed again. He knew one Indian who wouldn't scowl at him today. In his pack he carried a letter to the old Indian woman, Maconaquah, from her brother back in Pennsylvania. She received many letters from her white relatives since she had been reunited with them two years ago. It always made Miller feel good to watch her as he read them aloud to her. Her aged, stoical face was transformed by her smiles into much happier, softer lines. He could almost see the girl she once was.

Maconaquah heard the dogs barking and stood by her cabin door, watching as Miller splashed across the Mississinewa River. When she recognized the rider, she waved and walked to meet him by the tree where he hitched his horse. Greeting him by name, she made fast the reins as Miller rummaged in his saddlebag.

Seeing the letter, Maconaquah's stoic features softened considerably. She looked almost cheerful as she indicated the bench outside the door.

"Shingpiloh" (come sit), she said, reaching for the letter that Miller was holding out. Holding it for some moments, she carefully examined the handwriting and the quality of paper itself before handing it back to Miller, with a smile. "Now read, please," she indicated in the Miami tongue both understood. Maconaquah closed her eyes to listen to her brother's words from so far away.

Miller interpreted Joseph's letter slowly, extending the magic as long as possible. When he was finished, Maconaquah blinked open her eyes and gazed at him in wonderment.

"My blood brother coming to visit with two daughters? Show me the words."

Miller carefully pointed out the words and their meanings, until Maconaquah had the letter memorized. Now she could "read" it to the family. Preparations must be made. She instructed Miller to answer the letter, telling her brother they would be made welcome.

It took eighteen days of travel for Joseph and his daughters, Hannah and Harriet, to reach Peru from Wilkes-Barre, Pennsylvania. They traveled by stagecoach, railroad cars, canal boats and steamship northwest through Pennsylvania and New York, across Lake Erie, and then southwest through Ohio and Indiana.

Joseph's daughter, Hannah, kept a journal of the 48-day trip to Deaf Man's Village, on the banks of the Mississinewa River, in Indiana. Once there, she noted that the interior of the cabin had all the necessities. One room contained the cooking utensils; in the other were the table and dishes. There were six beds in the house, along with several splint-bottomed chairs and a looking glass. The Slocums were impressed with the fine detailed beading and applique on clothing hanging on pegs. Another surprise was the array of beautifully worked silver jewelry. They were obviously earrings, broaches and necklaces. The detail work was scrupulously, and very artistically, done by loving hands, they noticed.

Hannah described her Aunt Frances as being

...of small stature, not very much bent, with her gray hair clubbed behind in calico, tied with worsted ferret. Her eyes were clear and spritely for one of her age. Her face was wrinkled and weatherbeaten but not as dark as she would expect from her age. She had a scar on her left cheek received at an Indian dance. Her dress was a blue calico short gown, a white mackinaw blanket, a fold of blue broadcloth lapped around her, red cloth leggins and buckskin moccasins...

Along with Miller, Mr. Fulwiler and Mr. Saylor were there to interpret. The family had a delightful time getting acquainted with each other. For supper, her Indian relatives spread a cloth on the table and served a very comfortable meal of fried venison, tea, and shortcake.

Hannah was fascinated by her cousins:

...Aunt Frances' youngest daughter, O-zah-shin-quah, is small and quiet. Her children are Kip-pe-no-quah, Corn Tassel; Wap-pa-no-se-a, Blue Corn; Kim-on-tak-quah, Young Panther.

...Eldest daughter, Ke-ke-na-kush-wa, meaning Cut Finger, was large in size, smart, active, and observing. Her daughter by a previous marriage had recently been poisoned by the family of an Indian whom Maconaquah had rejected as a husband for her. Ke-ke-na-kush-wa is presently married to Captain Jean Baptiste Brouillette. They have no children...Captain Brouillette provides for the family very well by supplying game and cultivating the fields of corn and hay. He also chops the wood, which is unusual for an Indian.

...Their house is enclosed with a common worm fence, with some outhouses principally built of logs. A never-failing spring of excellent water is near the door, with a house over it. They have between fifty and sixty horses, one hundred hogs, seventeen head of cattle, also geese and chickens. There are six men's saddles and one side saddle of the most costly kind.

...The women's dresses are richly embroidered with silver broaches; seven and eight rows of broaches as closely as they can be put together. My aunt had several pairs of silver earrings in her ears; her daughters had perhaps a dozen apiece.

Harriet dressed in Indian costume to please Ke-ke-na-kush-wa, who told her she looked just like the daughter who had been poisoned. She asked Harriet to stay and take the place of her deceased child.

"Ke-ke-na-kush-wa," Harriet said slowly, faltering over the unfamiliar syllables, "I am honored, but as much as I am enjoying my visit, I cannot live here. I must return to my home."

"You would miss your friends," Ke-ke-na-kush-wa said sadly. "Like Maconaquah, you would be a fish out of water."

"That is right. Exactly right," Harriet answered, taking her cousin's hand. "But we will always be family. Nothing can change that."

After a four-day visit, the Slocums traveled home by the southern route. Reaching the Ohio River by stage coach and canal boat, they boarded a river boat for Pittsburgh, Pennsylvania. The boat was frequently grounded by low water and finally had to be evacuated near Wheeling, Virginia (West Virginia was still a part of Virginia at that time). From Wheeling, they traveled to Wilkes-Barre by coach, rail, and boat. The return trip took a total of twenty-five days. Hannah concluded her journal by noting that they had traveled 2,000 miles in seven weeks at a total cost of $387.69 1/2.

While still in Indiana, Joseph had sent a message to George Winter, an artist who had recently settled in Logansport, Indiana, requesting him to come to Deaf Man's Village and paint a portrait of Frances. Maconaquah was reluctant to have a "likeness" made of herself, since Indian culture likened it to the taking out of ones spirit. Her faith and trust in her brother, Joseph, must have been very strong by then, for Maconaquah did consent to sit for the portrait by George Winter.

Winter was an artist born and educated in England, but he had come to America as a young man. Believing that he was a witness to the passing of the traditional Indian way of life, he had spent many years painting scenes of that life.

Knowing of the Indians' reluctance to have their likeness put onto paper and that Maconaquah had probably consented to sit for him just to please her brother, Winter knew he would have to work fast. Just by sketching the details at the scene, he could complete the picture onto canvas back in his Logansport (Indiana) studio later on.

Maconaquah, begrudgingly, sat for two hours while Winter made his sketches. Later on, he recorded in his journal the following recollection of that moment: "Frances looked upon her likeness with complacency. Kick-ke-se-quah (ke-ke-na-kush-wa) eyed it approvingly, yet suspiciously - it was a mystery. The widowed daughter, O-shaw-se-quah (O-zah-shin-quah), would not look upon it, but turned away from it abruptly when I presented it to her for her inspection, as though some evil surrounded it.

I could but feel as by intuition, that my absence would be hailed as a joyous relief to the family."

Indeed, as Winter was making further sketches of the homestead, Maconquah ordered him off the premises. He had enough material, however, to make many finished pictures in oils and watercolors back in his studio. The entire George Winter collection is now the property of the Tippecanoe County Historical Association, of Lafayette,

Indiana.

Maconaquah's worst fears were realized when tribal leaders sold the last of the Miami's Great Reserve to the Americans in the Treaty of 1840. By the terms of the treaty, all Miamis who had not been awarded land, in that and other treaties, were required to move to a reservation in Kansas within five years.

"Since this section of land was legally given to your daughters in 1838, you might have to go to Kansas, too," James Miller explained to Maconaquah.

"I won't go," Maconaquah said defiantly. "I promised Shepoconah I would never leave this land. I must be buried by him and our sons." She wrung her wrinkled hands. "What can I do?"

"I reckon I better write Joseph," he answered. If I remember correctly, his son, Jonathan, is a lawyer. Maybe he'll know what to do."

Jonathan went into action immediately. He made up a petition, requesting exemption for Maconaquah and twenty-one other members of her Indian family, which included not only children, but grandchildren, husbands, cousins, nieces and nephews. Addressed to the United States Congress, the petition appealed for exemption because of her advanced age. It pointed out that she'd lived most of her life as an Indian but had recently been reunited with her white family. If she was sent far away to Kansas she might never see them again.

Congressman Samuel Sample and Alphonso A. Cole, a Miami County, Indiana, attorney, sent high recommendations for passage of the petition. The Hon.

Benjamin Bidlack, representing the Wyoming District of Pennsylvania, made an impressive speech before the House of Representatives, urging its passage. A joint resolution was presented to the Senate by Mr. White, Chairman of the Committee on Indian Affairs. The petition was approved on March 3, 1845, just a year before the deadline for the Miami's removal to Kansas.

Maconaquah had spent much time thinking about how to protect her Indian family while she awaited the outcome of the petition. Wisely, she accepted that the hunting ways of the Indian life were gone forever. They must live like the white people and get along with them, whether they liked it or not. To do this, they would need help. As soon as she learned she could remain at Deaf Man's Village, she had James Miller write to Isaac at his home in Bellevue, Ohio. She requested her brother to visit her as soon as possible to discuss a matter of great urgency.

Maconaquah had listened carefully to Isaac's many letters, telling her about his family. She believed that his youngest son, George, would be the best person to live at Deaf Man's Village and teach them all how to get along in the white man's world.

"I will adopt him," she said to Isaac. He will share my fortune equally with my daughters."

"But he's the one I've picked to live with me and care for my interests in my old age," Isaac protested.

"You know I was taken away when I was a little child and had no care from my people," Maconaquah said craftily, "while you had a father's and mother's care, and all their property. I have no sons - and much which needs looking after."

"I don't know if George would be willing to resettle way out here," Isaac said, giving way a little. "He's married now and had planned to stay in Bellevue." He was silent for what seemed like a long time. "If he is willing, I will give my consent," he finally said.

Isaac feared that his own reservations might influence George, so he merely informed his son that Aunt Frances wanted him to come out to Peru for the land sales. George was surprised and dismayed by Frances' offer. Living among the Indians was not what he had in mind as his life's work, but Frances was insistent. Finally, George agreed to talk it over with his wife before making a final decision.

When the annuities (payments for the Indians' lands) were distributed, Maconaquah kept her word and divided her share between her daughters and George. Before George returned to Bellevue, Maconaquah gave him a pony, with saddle and bridle, a pair of beaded moccasins, and some dried venison for his trip. As far as she was concerned, this act of giving and accepting consummated the adoption, according to tribal law.

George was a devout Baptist and looked on Maconaquah's request as a challenge to serve not only his family, but mankind itself. After much agonizing, he and his wife, Eliza, decided they must go to live with his Aunt Frances and her people on the banks of the Mississinewa river.

George returned to Indiana in January of 1846. He bought eighty acres of land near Deaf Man's Village, and built a fine cabin. In November, he brought Eliza and their infant daughter, Mary Cordelia, along with all their wordily possessions, to their new home. They intended to spend the rest of their lives with the Indians.

George immediately set out to learn the Miami language so he could talk directly with his relatives. He spent long hours that first winter talking with Maconaquah and reading the Bible to her. Eliza wrote:

> ...We weren't sure how much she understood, but she paid strict attention to all he said. Frances used to come to my house and watch me work. Her daughter and she used to admire my quilts and other things about the house.

Maconaquah was especially delighted with Mary Cordelia. The baby's dark auburn hair was the same color as the young Maconaquah's and Grandfather Jonathan's. She even had the same dark brown spot on the back of her head. This child, Maconaquah believed, would take her place in the world when she was gone. Maconaquah decided to give Mary Cordelia her most precious possession - her name. The baby was just nine months old when Maconaquah's daughters and grandchildren began to call her Mingiah, for "mother," and Macomah, for "grandmother."

At peace with herself, her white family, and the Great Spirit, Frances Slocum, known for most of her long life as Maconaquah, died the following year, on March 6, 1847.

George Winter's description of Deaf Man's Village:

"The sun was now on the decline, and... after a warm yet leisure walk of nine miles, I came upon a high bank, at the ford of the Mississinewa, where on the opposite bank the cabin of 'Ma-con-a-qua', and Deaf-man's village presented themselves to my view.

The river at this point was but a few rods in width, and very low,. But clear. The village confronted in a parallel line the bank upon which I stood. The river view looked eastwardly, was bounded by a graceful bend presenting a pleasant view-with the few cabins upon the bank, which converged nearly to a point where the bank of the opposite side curved so gracefully...

'The Wigwam' upon the Mississinawa at the Deafman's village where the Captive was discovered by her surviving relatives, was a large double log cabin of comfortable capacity - such as characterized the thrifty farmer's home in the West. A smaller cabin was attached to it in which a very aged squaw lived. There was also a small bark hut, separated at a distance from the main 'log', of a few rods..."

Deafman's Village by George Winter
Tippecanoe County Historical Association, Lafayette, Indiana. Gift of Mrs. Cable G. Ball

Log Cabin by George Winter
Tippecanoe County Historical Association, Lafayette, Indiana. Gift of Mrs. Cable G. Ball

EPILOGUE

George Slocum, along with his family, lived and worked with his cousins on the banks of the Mississinewa River until his death fourteen years later.

Captain Brouillette and Peter Bondy, O-zah-shin-quah's last husband, proved to be eager and able students. From George, they learned better methods of farming and medicine, along with an understanding of Christianity. Both men, in turn, devoted the rest of their lives to helping their fellow Indians adapt to a new way of life, to insure their survival.

Many books have been written about Frances' life, two lengthy poems, and many magazine articles and narrations in at least thirteen county and state histories. Some of the earlier authors actually interviewed Slocum family members to obtain first-hand facts, and there remains a wealth of journals, letters and diaries.

Faulty memories and authors' efforts to show their own views of Frances' situation have created many different versions of her story. For example, some writers stressed the brutality and heathenish ways of Indian life, while others have emphasized the intelligence and highly religious mores of the Native Americans.

In addition to discrepancies of fact, there abounds a variety of spellings of the Indian names. Since the Miamis had no written language, writers spelled names and words as they sounded to them. The English and French names of Indians were given to them when they were baptized into the Christian faith. Some Indians even adopted military titles of persons they admired.

In 1899, James F. Stutesman visited the "Bundy Burying

Ground," as the graveyard at Deaf Man's Village was known locally. He was appalled that the graves were largely unmarked and contacted Slocum family members back East. A committee was formed, money raised, and an appropriate marker ordered.

This was strictly a Slocum project, however, as Maconaquah's descendants, true to their Indian heritage and customs, did not believe grave markers were necessary. They knew where their ancestors were buried. Who else would be interested, except vandals?

On May 17, 1900, over two thousand persons witnessed the dedication of the white bronze monument to Maconaquah and her beloved Shepoconah, enclosed within an iron fence. It remained there for many years until the entire graveyard was moved to higher ground across the Mississinewa when the river was dammed in 1967, flooding the lowlands.

Long after Maconaquah joined Shepoconah in the Spirit World, her descendants remained active in promoting Miami recognition in the state of Indiana. A grandson, Camillus Bundy, became chief of the Miami Indians who had stayed in Indiana. It was he who founded the tribe's legal organization, called "Miami Nation of Indians in Indiana." Bundy and Gabriel Godfroy, who married Moconaquah's favorite granddaughter, Elizabeth, spent their adult lives in court battles, trying to force the U.S. government to live up to treaty agreements.

Great-grandson Clarence Godfroy (1880-1962) and Ross Bundy (1879-1963) trained young men of the tribe in the traditional hunting and fishing methods used by their ancestors. They were also the last Miamis who could speak the native tongue fluently. They became great storytellers, passing the legends on to the next generation. In the 1920s and 1930s they raised money by traveling around northern Indiana with a troupe of other tribal members, presenting Indian dances and customs.

Few private individuals have been honored by so many permanent memorials. Indiana maintains Frances Slocum State Forest, north of the Mississinewa Lake, which was formed when the river was dammed in 1967. At the site of that dam is the Frances Slocum Recreation Area, featuring Lost Sister Trail, one and one half miles of conservation/education hiking trail. The old Bundy Burying Ground was relocated near that area, and within its enclosure lay the graves of Maconaquah, Shepoconah, and other family members. It is owned today by the Miami Nation.

The Frances Slocum Trail (in places called Old Slocum Trail) takes motorists along the south side of the lake between Peru and Marion, where the Miamis lived for over 150 years. A shopping center, bank, and trailer park in that area are named for Frances Slocum. A city park in Peru and the Bunker Hill School Corporation carry the name Maconaquah.

In Pennsylvania, a plaque at the entrance to the Wyoming Historical and Geological Society Museum in Wilkes-Barre briefly relates the legend of Frances Slocum. Abraham Creek, the waterway along which the Indians fled with their young captives in 1778, flows through what is now known as Frances Slocum State Park, twelve miles north of Wilkes-Barre.

At the site of the old Slocum homestead in Wilkes-Barre stands an abandoned factory, but across the street children enjoy a playground donated by a Slocum descendant in Frances' memory. When Chief Tuck Horse carried Frances off so long ago, over the very same ground, he couldn't have imagined he was carrying her into the pages of history.

BIBLIOGRAPHY

Frohman, Charles E., <u>A History of Sandusky and Erie County</u>, Ohio Historical Society, 1965

Harvey, Oscar J., <u>A History of Wilkes-Barre and Wyoming Valley</u>, Vol. 2, Page 1088, Chap. XVIII, Pages 1113-1144, Smith-Bennett Publishing Co., Wilkes-Barre, PA., 1909

Harvey, Oscar J., <u>A History of Wilkes-Barre</u>, copyrighted May, 1909. Published by Raeder Press, Wilkes-Barre, PA..

Indiana Historical Society, <u>The Journals and Indian Paintings of George Winter</u>, Page 39, Indianapolis, IN, 1948

<u>Indians and a Changing Frontier: The Art of George Winter</u>, a catalog of George Winter's paintings and journals, compiled by Sarah E. Cooke and Rachel B. Ramadhyani. Published in Indianapolis, Indiana, 1993, by the Indiana Historical Society, in cooperation with the Tippecanoe County Historical Association.

The Lewis Publishing Company, <u>History of Miami County, Indiana</u>, Vol. I, Chap. IV, Pages 52-66, New York, 1914

Meginness, John F., Biography of Frances Slocum, <u>The Lost</u>

Sister of the Wyoming, Williamsport, PA, 1891

Peeke, Heuson L., History of Erie County, Vol. I, Lewis
  Publishing Co., 1916

Rafert, Stewart, The Hidden Community: The Miami
  Indians of Indiana, 1879-1973, University of Delaware,
  1982

Smithsonian Institution, Handbook of North American
  Indians, Northeast, Vol. 15, Wash. D.C., 1978

Weslager, C. A., The Delaware Indians, Rutgers University
  Press, New Brunswick, NJ, 1972

Winger, Otho, The Lost Sister of the Miamis, The Elgin
  Press, Elgin, IL, 1938

INDEX